Praise for D. Jac

Unbridle

"A hot, steamy, erotic romance myst... and turns, great characters and an unforgettable story that I was completely invested in. It was difficult to put the book down and I thoroughly enjoyed the whole experience of reading it!" —*LESBIReviewed*

Blades of Bluegrass

"Both lead characters, Britt and Teddy, were well developed and likeable. I also really enjoyed the supporting characters, like E.B., and the warm, familiar atmosphere the author managed to create at Story Hill Farm."—*Melina Bickard, Librarian, Waterloo Library (UK)*

Ordinary Is Perfect

"There's something incredibly charming about this small town romance, which features a vet with PTSD and a workaholic marketing guru as a fish out of water in the quiet town. But it's the details of this novel that make it shine."—*Pink Heart Society*

Take a Chance

"I really enjoyed the character dynamic with this book of two very strong independent women who aren't looking for love but fall for the one they already love…The chemistry and dynamic between these two is fantastic and becomes even more intense when their sexual desires take over."—*Les Rêveur*

Dragon Horse War

"Leigh writes with an emotion that she in turn gives to the characters, allowing us insight into their personalities and their very souls. Filled with fantastic imagery and the down-to-earth flaws that are sometimes the characters' greatest strengths, this first *Dragon Horse War* is a story not to be missed. The writing is flawless, the story, breath-taking—and this is only the beginning."—*Lambda Literary Review*

"The premise is original, the fantasy element is gripping but relevant to our times, the characters come to life, and the writing is phenomenal. It's the author's best work to date and I could not put it down."—*Melina Bickard, Librarian, Waterloo Library (UK)*

"Already an accomplished author of many romances, Leigh takes on fantasy and comes up aces…So, even if fantasy isn't quite your thing, you should give this a try. Leigh's backdrop is a world you already recognize with some slight differences, and the characters are marvelous. There's a villain, a love story, and…ah yes, 'thar be dragons.'"—*Out in Print: Queer Book Reviews*

"This book is great for those that like romance with a hint of fantasy and adventure."—*The Lesbrary*

"Skin Walkers" in *Women of the Dark Streets*

"When love persists through many lifetimes, there is always the potential magic of reunion. Climactically resplendent!"—*Rainbow Book Reviews*

Swelter

"I don't think there is a single book D. Jackson Leigh has written that I don't like…I recommend this book if you want a nice romance mixed with a little suspense."—*Kris Johnson, Texas Library Association*

"This book is a great mix of romance, action, angst, and emotional drama…The first half of the book focuses on the budding relationship between the two women, and the gradual revealing of secrets. The second half ramps up the action side of things…There were some good sexy scenes, and also an appropriate amount of angst and introspection by both women as feelings more than just the physical started to surface."—*Rainbow Book Reviews*

Call Me Softly

"*Call Me Softly* is a thrilling and enthralling novel of love, lies, intrigue, and Southern charm."—*Bibliophilic Book Blog*

Touch Me Gently

"D. Jackson Leigh understands the value of branding, and delivers more of the familiar and welcome story elements that set her novels apart from other authors in the romance genre."—*Rainbow Reader*

Every Second Counts

"Her prose is clean, lean, and mean—elegantly descriptive."—*Out in Print: Queer Book Reviews*

Riding Passion

"The sex was always hot and the relationships were realistic, each with their difficulties. The technical writing style was impeccable, ranging from poetic to more straightforward and simple. The entire anthology was a demonstration of Leigh's considerable abilities."—*2015 Rainbow Awards*

By the Author

Romance

Call Me Softly

Touch Me Gently

Hold Me Forever

Swelter

Take a Chance

Ordinary Is Perfect

Blades of Bluegrass

Unbridled

Forever Comes in Threes

Here for You

When Tomorrow Comes

Cherokee Falls Series

Bareback

Long Shot

Every Second Counts

Dragon Horse War Trilogy

The Calling

Tracker and the Spy

Seer and the Shield

Short story collection

Riding Passion

When Tomorrow Comes

by

D. Jackson Leigh

2024

WHEN TOMORROW COMES

ISBN 13: 978-1-63679-557-7

This Trade Paperback Original Is Published By
Bold Strokes Books, Inc.
P.O. Box 249
Valley Falls, NY 12185

First Edition: February 2024

Credits
Editor: Shelley Thrasher
Production Design: Stacia Seaman
Cover Design by Tammy Seidick

Acknowledgments

As always, thanks to my awesome editor, Shelley Thrasher. I can always trust her to make my stories better.

Chapter One

The cloudless blue sky and the lush green lawn dotted with pink and white flowering trees was a sharp contrast to the funeral procession disgorging passengers clad mostly in black and solemn shades of gray.

Teague Maxwell stood uphill from the gravesite, apart from the mourners gathering for a final farewell. She spent little time with her extended family, but at least half of them had been irritatingly attentive to her at the funeral, while the other half cast furtive glances her way. Nephew Donnie was thinking about getting a pig for a pet, so could he come to her house and meet her pig? Aunt Roberta was so sorry she hadn't checked in to see if Teague was doing okay since her parents died. Cousin Leon wanted to know if he could drop by and see what interesting project she was currently working on.

Her extended family mostly treated her like an oddity, and none had ever visited her estate after her parents died. She didn't mind that they avoided her, since most of them were dull and stupid. So why did they want to pester her now? She was keeping her distance from those pesky relatives at the graveside and already had decided to skip the potluck gathering at her deceased cousin's home. She didn't like crowds. The funeral was okay because they sat in orderly rows. Her anxiety grew, though, when they were milling around her afterward. Too many people.

She closed her eyes and pulled in a long breath of pollen-laden spring air as numbers and symbols in one long, comforting equation filled her mind. The numbers still didn't add up, but she was close to a breakthrough and had learned over the years to listen to her intuition.

"Hello? Earth to Teague."

She jerked back from the bony fingers waving inches away from her face. "Aunt Margaret." She smiled and playfully swatted her great-aunt's hand away. "Maybe I was praying for my cousin's soul. Your interruption might keep him in purgatory for a millennium."

"Ha. You're an agnostic. You've never prayed in your life."

The irreverent, sometimes crotchety old woman was the one relative Teague did like. "Okay. I zoned out for a minute, thinking about work."

"Ha, more like the fifteen minutes it took for me to hobble up this hill without you noticing." Ninety-two years had shrunk and bent her great-aunt's petite frame and diminished her tolerance for social niceties, but they had failed to dull her razor-sharp mind. "NASA need a new toilet for that space station?"

Teague frowned. "Why would they need a new toilet design? The one they have works perfectly well."

Margaret shook her head. "I've always said God left out the part of your brain that recognizes humor and used that space in your skull to pack in more analytic cells."

"Those analytic brain cells help me solve problems nobody else can."

"Little use for modesty either, I see." Her aunt's chuckle assured her this was a tease, not a barb. "Your honesty is so refreshing." She held out her arms. "I know you don't like hugs, but I don't have many years left to steal them from you."

She steeled herself and stepped into her aunt's embrace, then relaxed as Margaret's deceptively strong arms tightened around her for a full minute. She didn't like people touching her, but firm, prolonged pressure could be strangely calming. Margaret knew that.

Teague had been diagnosed when a child as high-functioning on the autism scale. While she normally obsessed over adhering to the same daily routine, she also could lose herself in a project and forget to shower, eat, or sleep for days. And she had trouble recognizing emotions on the faces of other people. But she was okay with her idiosyncrasies. Most people accepted her quirks as side effects of her genius.

"I can't believe in this world of modern medicine, we still have family members succumbing to the Maxwell curse," Margaret said before releasing her.

While it wasn't unusual for some diseases to be inherited, most of the Maxwells had died of brain or aortic aneurysms. Teague shivered. The idea of a curse wasn't logical, but the fact that all died during the year following their fortieth birthday was tough to ignore. "Cousin Bernard was looking rather pale at the funeral service. I figure he's somewhere in his late thirties."

Margaret peered up at her. "How old are you?"

"I'll turn forty in a few days, but I'm not worried. I was adopted."

"Shit a brick."

Teague turned to Margaret, surprised at her rare use of profanity. "I beg your pardon?"

Margaret adjusted her broad-brimmed, lacy hat, then thumped her cane on the ground several times. "I can't believe your parents never talked to you about your biological parents," she said, still thumping her cane. "This entire family is a bunch of spineless idiots."

"Aunt Margaret." Teague narrowed her eyes and stared hard at her aunt. "What do you know that you aren't telling me?"

❖

Baye Cobb plucked the adventurous kitten from her shoulder. "Ow, little guy. Your claws are sharp." She put him on the floor next to his littermates while she watched. "Go play with your siblings." Her voice was stern but turned to giggles when the kitten pounced on another one and scrambled up her back again to rub his chin against her cheek. "No fair. Sucking up to me won't get you extra kibble."

"There you are! Damn it, Baye. Don't tell me you've taken in another litter. We're already overflowing with kittens." Baye's cousin, Libby, stood in the doorway of the room used to quarantine new feline arrivals until they could be tested for diseases.

Baye pulled the kitten from her shoulder again and cuddled him in her arms. "The guy said he was going to sell them to somebody who owns a really big snake if we didn't take them off his hands. What else could I do?"

"Really?" Libby eyed her suspiciously. "You could report him to animal control and turn the cats over to the county shelter."

Baye clutched the kitten tighter and began to gather the other four in her arms. She gave her cousin a beseeching look and squeezed out a single tear big enough to trickle down her cheek. She found *the tear* a valuable tool for getting what she wanted and could produce it on command. "I could never leave an animal at that nasty place. Besides, they'd kill them after a few weeks if they weren't adopted. You know that."

"I know it's almost noon, and you haven't finished the morning feeding."

"I was just about done when that guy showed up with the kittens, and I guess these little cuties distracted me." She began to gently place the kittens in a large wire crate that held a cuddly blanket and a small water bowl.

"You aren't almost done. You haven't taken care of at least half of the indoor animals, and none of the outdoor ones."

Oops. Libby must have built up an immunity to *the tear*. "I'll go finish now."

Libby seemed to deflate with a long, audible sigh and shook

her head. "Don't bother. I finished for you." She grabbed one of the kittens Baye hadn't corralled yet and sat on the floor to cuddle it. "We've spent the monthly allotment for animal food already, and all the utility bills are at least a month behind, not to mention what we owe the vet. The monthly allowance from the trust should be more than enough. What did you spend the money on?"

Baye hated that she was always disappointing people. "I don't know where all the money goes."

Libby put the kitten in the crate with the rest. "It's not just where the money's going. It's also not coming in. We knew from the beginning that the trust fund wouldn't cover all our expenses. That's why we filed to be a nonprofit, which we apparently excel at since we've never even met budget, much less made a profit."

When their lesbian, unmarried aunt died, she had left her twenty-acre farm to Baye, her only gay niece, and Libby, the only family member who hadn't given up hope Baye could learn to manage her ADHD impulsiveness. A trust fund provided them each a modest monthly allowance, and a third allotment paid her aunt's longtime gardener's salary and expenses to maintain the farm property. The acreage was too small to be profitable as a farm, so they embarked on Baye's dream of turning it into an animal-rescue center. They only needed to break even on the rescue center, but lately the operation expenses had been eating all the farm's allowance, plus their personal allotments.

"We've been getting lots of applications to adopt since I put up the website," Baye said, hoping to wiggle out of this uncomfortable conversation.

"Yes, because you did an awesome job building the website. You're crazy smart and creative, but it took you a year to finish it. Besides, the website's useless if you don't read the adoption applications and respond. They just keep piling up on the dining room table."

"We can look at them together after dinner."

Libby took Baye's hands in hers. "Honey, I love you, but you need to try to focus enough to finish at least one thing without me." Libby withdrew her hands. "Besides, I start a part-time job this afternoon. I have my own bills to pay."

Baye frowned. "You could save money if you moved into the farmhouse with me."

Libby shook her head. "No way. As much as I love you, I cannot live in your mess and clutter. I'd get tired of picking up your fast-food containers and doing all the housework, and I'd grow to resent you. I love you too much to let that happen."

Baye wanted to promise she'd clean up after herself, but she and Libby both knew she'd be distracted by a million other things after only a few weeks. She'd lost roommate after roommate because of week-old—sometimes month-old—fast-food containers and laundry covering every surface of the house. She loved a clean house, but she could never stay focused long enough to keep it that way. She nodded after Libby had so frankly declined her offer. Libby was one of the few real friends she had. She couldn't risk losing her, too. "Okay. I love you, too."

Libby stood and pulled on her hand for Baye to stand and accept a tight hug. "I'm going to work, and you should read and respond to some of those applications. We need the adoption fees to buy animal feed for the rest of the month and pay the utility bills so your electricity and gas aren't shut off again."

Baye released her cousin from their hug. "I promise I will."

When she glanced back at the playful kittens, Libby grabbed her hand. "I'll walk you back to the house so you can start on them now."

"Okay." The kittens would have to wait.

CHAPTER TWO

"Those laser eyes don't intimidate me." Aunt Margaret lowered her voice as the graveside service began a scant fifty yards below them. "Haven't you ever wondered about your birth parents?"

"Why should I?" Teague had found her parents adequate and even loved them in her own way, so she didn't want or need more.

"Because you're abnormally curious about everything, damn it." Margaret scowled up at her. "Why in God's name aren't you curious about your birth parents?"

"Because they are of no consequence. My adopted parents gave me food, shelter, security, adequate wealth, and enough room to be myself."

"Don't you worry about things like their medical history?"

"No. I have screened my own DNA, and it carries no markers for dementia, Alzheimer's, cancer, or other inherited diseases."

"DNA screening can't detect some things."

Realization began to dawn. "What do you know that I do not? What secret has been kept from me?"

"It's not my place to tell you, dear."

"Then who? You know Mom and Dad are gone, and I am an only child. Who does that leave?" Her voice was rising and her aggravation building. She took a deep breath and began rhythmically touching each fingertip to her thumbs, a diversion she'd learned to calm herself.

The funeral forgotten, Margaret hooked her arm in Teague's. "Walk me to your car and take me home before you have one of your famous meltdowns in the middle of Melvin's funeral. I'll tell you when we get to my house."

She balked. "Tell me now."

Margaret narrowed her eyes in a scowl. "Don't you sass me, young lady. Help me to your car."

Teague sighed. She would have a better chance at robbing Fort Knox than prying information from Margaret before she was ready. "Okay." She walked Margaret to her Jeep Cherokee, helped her inside, and then drove her home.

Once they arrived, Teague's finger-thumb touching escalated to rhythmic tapping of her fingers against her thigh while she waited for her great-aunt to remove her hat and ask her housekeeper to bring refreshments to them on the patio.

Margaret pulled a cashmere shawl around her shoulders. "Will you drag that table and our chairs into the sunlight, please, Teague?"

"We can sit inside if you are chilled." She seated Margaret, then took her own chair.

"No, no. I'm sure I'll shed the shawl as soon as the sun warms up my old bones." She surveyed her large, perfectly manicured gardens. "I do believe the roses are already growing buds. I can't wait for them to bloom."

Teague's impatience turned to anxiety, and she moved her hands to tap, tap, pause, tap, tap, tap her fingers on the arms of her chair. "What secret, Aunt Margaret? What is this big family skeleton everybody knows but me?" She was already mentally churning through any inherited diseases she hadn't been tested for. ALS? Nope. Tested negative for that, too.

"You're so curious about everything. I thought you would've figured out who birthed you by the time you were six years old."

"It was a closed adoption."

"There are other ways to find a parent, a brother, or a sister. Can't you track down lost family through DNA?"

"Yes, in some cases but—" Honestly, Teague hadn't sought out her birth parents because she didn't like people all that much, and she already had more family than she could deal with. Why look for more?

The conversation paused while Beverly, her aunt's longtime housekeeper, arranged a tea service and small trays of cookies and raw vegetables between them.

"Thank you, Beverly," Margaret said. "Would you like to join us?"

The housekeeper shook her head. "Nope. I know what you're talking about, and you're not going to mix me up in your family's mess." Beverly gave them a dismissive wave and returned to the house.

"Family mess?" Teague blinked at the figurative red flag waving before her eyes.

"There's no mess," Margaret said, calmly pouring tea for them. "Simply a lack of sharing."

"Then share with me now," she said, ignoring the teacup Margaret pushed toward her.

Margaret spooned sugar into her tea and stirred. And stirred.

"Aunt Margaret. Just spill it."

"Your birth father was your father's older half brother."

"What? Dad did not have an older brother."

"He did." Margaret sipped her tea. "Raymond was the product of an affair your grandfather had early in his marriage. He was raised by his mother outside our family but died shortly after his fortieth birthday."

Teague's mind usually worked at hyperspeed, but it felt suddenly mired in these new, confusing facts. "He died? Was it an accident? Cancer?"

Margaret laid her hand on Teague's forearm. "A brain aneurysm, dear."

Teague jumped up from her seat and paced the patio, flinging her arms upward in frustration. "Was nobody going to tell me that my father was really my uncle? That the next family gathering will likely to be my funeral?"

"I know this is a shock, but don't go off the deep end." Margaret sipped her tea. "I love this blend. What do you think of it?" She waved a dismissive hand. "Doesn't matter. I like it, so I'll ask Beverly to order some more."

Teague paused a second. "Tea? You want to talk about tea?" Teague gesticulated wildly as she spoke. "I could drop dead in the next month. I have to call my doctor. I need to get my life in order. I need to update my will and find good homes for my animals. What will happen to my estate?"

"Calm down. You're going to work yourself into one of your episodes."

Teague fought her rising anxiety. "I just found out I have a year or less to live."

"Nonsense. These are modern times with new medical advances every day."

"Easy for you to say. You are related by marriage, not blood."

"Amanda Teague Maxwell. You're a scientist. I can't believe you're buying into that stupid curse rumor. I think half of the family members who've died after turning forty caused their own aneurysm by stressing over that alleged curse, and you will too if you don't pull yourself together."

"I am going home." She headed toward the house.

"Wait, honey. I don't want you to leave here upset." Margaret rose from her chair.

Teague stopped, paced back to her, and initiated the hug she normally avoided. "I am not upset with you. Thank you for finally telling me, but I need to think, and I do that best at home."

❖

Baye eyed the tall stack of adoption applications. Some were months old, so the applicants likely had found pets at another rescue or local shelter. Libby was right. The number of dogs, cats, puppies, and kittens was almost tenfold the number they had expected the rescue would attract. She sighed, opened a can of supercharged energy drink, and began sorting the applications into three piles—those more than two months old, ones that might still be viable, and those with enough red flags to go straight into the trash. Two hours later, she threw her hands up and hunched over to gently bang her head against the tabletop.

"This is going to drive me crazy. Adopting out one animal at a time will never work."

The concept of running a rescue had seemed like a great one. Libby was reluctant, but they had used a huge piece of their trusts to convert the large barn into kennels and build a cathouse that contained a modest clinic for vet visits. The two buildings included reception and "playrooms," where prospective adopters could get to know the animals they hoped to adopt. Managing the building project was a ton of work, but Libby and John, the gardener-slash-groundskeeper, handled most of it, while Baye painted a beautiful mural on the face of the barn that identified the new venture as "Heavy Petting Animal Rescue." She modified the design to produce business cards, print T-shirts and souvenir mugs, and use as the logo for their website.

Everything was fantastic at first. Baye recruited a network of volunteer fosters to keep the farm's animal census to a reasonable number, plus a handful of high school and college kids to help at the farm. She was very sociable and loved working with people and animals.

She wasn't great, however, at keeping appointments, delivering feed and supplies to the volunteer fosters, or managing her young volunteers. Most of the fosters eventually left to help other, better organized rescue groups. And she wanted so desperately for the teen volunteers to like her, word got around that she let them do things their parents forbade—smoke cigarettes, vape, and play video games all night. Her house had become a hangout for kids who had no interest in working in the kennels, and those teens ran off those who did want to work with the animals rather than goof off. Libby ran off the loafers after the workers quit.

At least during those first years she was awesome at organizing adoption events. After a while, however, she earned a reputation for poor communication with the stores offering space for the events and skimpy cleanup afterward, so the store managers instead began to book other, more reliable rescue groups.

She drummed her fingers on the table. Screw 'em. Those stores had too many rules anyway. She brightened. She would plan a huge adoption event here at the farm. Yeah. That would work. She could hire a face-painting artist and maybe rent one of those big slides for the kids, and get a DJ to play music. People could fill out an adoption application online in advance and bring it with them to avoid a bottleneck of potential adopters completing paperwork at the event. Baye raised her arms over her head and mimicked the noise of a crowd cheering her idea. She needed to text Libby. This would be so great!

She stood. "Problem solved for now." She grabbed her phone and began to tap out a long explanation of her idea to Libby, who didn't answer because she was working at her new job. "No matter," Baye said cheerfully, grinning and indulging in a few celebratory dance moves. "I better check on the kittens."

❖

A Sicilian donkey with one long ear and a second half ear galloped along the other side of the driveway fence to keep pace with Teague's vehicle, his raucous brays alerting the rest of the estate to her return. A half dozen chickens, a llama, a goat and her two kids, three sheep, and a mountain of a dog emerged from the small barn, surrounding pastures, and expansive yard. She drove carefully around the house to park outside her four-car garage and got out to greet the convergence of animals. The donkey stopped braying long enough to use his thick lips to unlatch the pasture gate and swing the gate open for himself and others, and Teague braced herself for his affectionate head-butt that was always part of his enthusiastic greeting.

"Asset, hello. Yes. I am home. Thank you for announcing my arrival." She grabbed four cloth bags from the back seat, having filled them with various fruits and vegetables at her favorite roadside stand on the way home from Margaret's house, and held out an apple to the donkey. "Stuff that loud mouth of yours with this."

She led the others back into the pasture while handing out vegetables and fruits to most, plus a foot-long rawhide bone for Snow, a Great Pyrenees mix, and his terrier sidekick, Badger, to share. The goats and llama gobbled up the raw turnips and collards, and she threw out a few handfuls of cracked corn for the chickens. Geese honked their greeting but apparently were satisfied grazing down by the pond inside the pasture.

"Where is Flower?" Teague surveyed the grounds, her gaze snagging on the sunroom door sliding open. A furry capuchin face appeared briefly, then disappeared back in the house. "Cappie, you better get out here. Have you and Flower been watching my television again?"

She started for the house, only to be met by a mass of furiously flapping blue and gold feathers. The macaw landed a few feet away and waddled toward her. "Nobody home. Check the barn. Nobody home."

Teague held out cluster of grapes. "Want to think that over, Mac?"

The large parrot tilted his head, eyeing the grapes as if considering them. "Bad pig. Bad monkey. Lock him up. Lock him up."

Teague handed over the grapes to her informant. "Aha. So Cappie let Flower in the house?"

"Bad monkey, pick the lock. Ticktock, pick the lock." Mac's tattling dissolved into indistinguishable satisfied noises as the parrot clutched his third grape with his foot and delicately peeled away the skin to nibble at the juicy pulp.

Cappie reappeared in the doorway, then ran across the lawn to snatch a few of Mac's grapes. He watched Teague and stayed just out of her reach while he stuffed several grapes into his cheeks and scurried back to the sunroom.

"Thief!" The feathers on Mac's neck stood out like a lion's mane as he spread his wings in a threatening gesture. It was a game with them. Since both ate a similar diet, they were constantly stealing from each other. He dragged what was left of his grape cluster a few feet away, as if that could stop the lightning-quick monkey. "Time out. Time out."

"Yeah, yeah. That tree-climbing devil is going to get a lot of time-out in his cage if I find Flower in the pantry again." Her growled words didn't seem to bother her menagerie. Her bark rarely had any bite behind it. Still, she stomped into the house and gasped. The kitchen counters and floor were covered with flour, uncooked pasta, rice, condiments, cereal, and a ton of other foodstuffs. It looked like twenty monkeys had held a party, and a two-hundred-pound pig was in the middle of the mess, its snout stuck in a huge jar of peanut butter.

"Flower!"

The pig dislodged the peanut-butter jar with a squeal and scrambled around behind the large kitchen island. Cappie, the monkey, bounded into the house and ricocheted off the sofa in the sitting area next to the kitchen to leap and swing from one of several play ropes dangling from the beams of the vaulted ceiling. He kept up a scolding chatter until Teague pointed to him. "You are toast, too, Monkey King. I do not think that Flower can open the latch on the pantry and pull all that food down from the shelves."

Cappie, however, wasn't intimidated or showing any remorse for the mess, while Flower peeked at Teague from behind the kitchen island. Her pig brain apparently determined her owner wasn't too angry, and she approached, making happy little grunting noises and swishing her short tail rapidly back and forth.

Teague sighed. She should be angry at them, but, damn it, they were just too adorable, and she was suddenly aware her time with them might be short. A heavy blanket of sadness seemed to drape over her. What would become of her annoying, beloved pets?

Chapter Three

Baye showed another family into the cathouse. "Y'all play with them as much as you want. If you have any questions, just find me, my cousin Libby, or one of the volunteers wearing a yellow Heavy Petting T-shirt."

She headed outside to check in with Libby, who was manning the adoption tables where people were filling out paperwork to adopt an animal they'd chosen. "How's it going?"

Libby looked up from the application she was reviewing. "Are you okay adopting out cats to be barn cats? A lady here wants to adopt a mama cat and her entire litter of four."

"You have to watch out for anyone who wants to adopt several, especially kittens. They could be someone looking for a meal for some huge snake."

"I can assure you that Mary Anne is not looking for snake food."

Baye turned to find a tall, dark-haired woman with arresting brown eyes and the longest lashes she'd ever seen that weren't fake. She smiled and held out her hand. "Hi. I'm Baye Cobb, and this is my first cousin, Libby. We own Heavy Petting."

The woman nodded but ignored Baye's hand. "Teague Maxwell." She pointed to the property adjacent to Heavy Petting. "I am your neighbor."

"Ah. The mysterious neighbor with the impressive menagerie."

"Have they been bothering you?"

"No. Not at all. They come down to the fence sometimes, like now, to mooch a few treats." She pointed to the fence where Asset, Flower, three sheep, and three goats were holding court with a small group of children feeding them dog biscuits. "But they're no problem. People seem to think they're just part of the adoption festival." Baye swept her arm in an arc to indicate the bounce tent and inflatable slide she'd rented for the event, and the ice-cream truck she'd hired to hand out free icy treats.

"Adoption festival?" Teague surveyed the good-sized crowd. "I thought this was a child's birthday party or something. I did not mean to impose, but I stopped by to speak to Mary Anne Beck after I recognized her truck."

"Birthday parties. What a brilliant idea. We could book birthday parties here, and the kids could play with the dogs and kittens as part of the party." Baye bounced on her toes a few times as her ideas began to flow. "It could be extra income for the rescue. We could offer for the birthday kid to request donations to the rescue rather than gifts."

She widened her eyes and clapped her hands to her cheeks as a sudden epiphany hit her. "We could make up cards with the animals' photos on them and let the kids pick a dog or cat to benefit from their donation. Plus, I bet we'd adopt out more than a few dogs and cats when the parents come to pick up their kids from the party."

"You know Ms. Beck?" As usual, Libby interceded to bring Baye's focus back to the original conversation.

"Yes. She is the owner of River Run Riding Stables. I leased a horse there for occasional riding until a few years ago. She just added a second barn to her property so she could keep her schooling horses separate from the show horses she boards and trains."

"Schooling horses?" The idea of a bunch of horses in a schoolroom intrigued Baye.

"Horses and ponies that are gentle and experienced enough

to use for teaching children and some adults how to ride," Teague said. "I imagine she wants the cats for the new barn, to keep mice out of the horse feed."

"Oh." Libby nodded.

"Any cats living in her fancy barns would have cozy beds, be fed every time the horses were, get regular veterinary care, and lots of attention from the kids who hang out there before and after their riding lessons. Mary Anne is also very committed to neutering, so there would not be any unwanted pregnancies."

Libby smiled and placed a large checkmark in the upper corner of Mary Anne's application. "I'll go let her know her application is approved."

"I'll do it." Baye snatched the paper up before Libby rose from her chair. She wanted a chance to get to know her intriguing neighbor. "We have several litters. I can help her pick out one." She gestured to two families standing by to check out with the pet they'd selected. "I think you have other customers waiting." She turned back to Teague. "I believe Ms. Beck is in the cathouse. You can come with me if you still want to speak with her."

"Thank you." Teague was normally oblivious to attractive women unless they were direct about their interest in her, because her brain was always working in the background to solve her latest project challenge, and the rest of her attention was focused on her very active animal family. But she was curiously drawn to this hazel-eyed beauty and her strange energy. She'd been aware the elderly woman who had lived there had died, then watched the small farm when it was crawling with building contractors. She'd even given a large anonymous donation online when she discovered the farm was being repurposed as an animal rescue. She had not, however, felt compelled to meet her new neighbors. But she was here now and nervously followed Baye through the milling crowd.

"I never met anyone who lives in a mansion," Baye said. "It looks huge from the outside. Do you live there alone?"

"No." Conversations with people she did not know well were awkward for Teague. Most seemed to be put off by her stilted speech and lack of eye contact.

Baye stopped their trek to the cathouse and grasped Teague's forearm. "I'm sorry. I don't mean to be intrusive. You didn't have to answer that question. I sometimes forget that some people don't like to talk about themselves the way I do."

Teague stilled at Baye's touch on the bare skin of her forearm. She normally bristled when a stranger invaded her personal space, but Baye's touch was warm and light. She managed a glance into those hazel eyes that seemed to go green in the sunlight. "I have a live-in house manager, and"—she gestured to the fence where her pets were still mooching dog biscuits and ice cream from the delighted children—"my rather eclectic collection of animal friends."

Baye's eyes widened. "How many animals do you have?"

Teague again gestured to the fence. "The Sicilian donkey is Asset. The pot-bellied pig is Flower. The goats are Miss Abigail and her kids, Tater and Tot. The sheep are the Fluffies—Cotton, Crochet and Yarn. Lucky is the llama lurking nearby. He won't come to the fence because he's wary of strangers. Then there's Cappie, my capuchin-monkey terrorist, and Mac, a blue-and-gold macaw. Miss Hennie is the boss hen of a small flock of free-range chickens, and two large rabbits in the barn graze loose at night."

"Wow. Don't you have any traditional pets? You know, a dog or cat?"

"Leo is a very large and lazy Maine coon cat. Snow is a Great Pyrenees mix, and his terrier sidekick is Badger, who helps Leo keep my barn free of mice."

Baye stared at her. "So, I guess you're not here to adopt another animal?"

Teague sighed and stared at the ground. She was still

digesting and wasn't ready to share the news of her curse. "No. I am not. I wanted to talk to Mary Anne about taking some of my animals if something happens to me."

Baye blinked. "Are you expecting something to happen?"

Teague shifted uncomfortably under Baye's concerned gaze. "Nobody can know what the future holds. I like to be prepared. Connie, my house manager, says it is one of my quirks."

Baye's hand tightened briefly on Teague's arm before she released her. "Not a bad quirk to have, I'd say."

Teague glanced up and was again struck by those mesmerizing eyes. "Thank you. I do not understand why, but my insistence on always having a plan irritates many people." She shrugged and, before she could stop herself, confessed to this stranger, "I do not make friends easily."

Baye's smile blazed. "Well, neighbor, we certainly have that in common." She caught Teague's hand and tugged her toward the cathouse. "I think you and I could become good friends."

❖

They sat on the carpeted floor with cats and kittens playing around them. Playing with animals was in Teague's comfort zone. She had always liked them better than people.

"I'm thinking this little gray mama and her two kittens will be perfect for the new barn," Mary Anne said. The mama cat purred in her lap, while the six-week-old kittens played nearby with an older kitten friend.

"That's wonderful," Baye said, her eyes pools of gloom. "Only…well, Jimmy will be very sad." She pointed to the older kitten. "He's the last of his litter. Their mother ran in front of a truck on the highway, and the guy who hit her managed to gather the kittens and bring them to us. Gray Mama sort of adopted little Jimmy into her litter after the other kittens were gone."

"Then you must take Jimmy along with the others," Teague

said, picking up the kitten in question and holding him to her cheek. "He has lost his mother and siblings. You cannot take his new family away from him."

"We can give you a special group price," Baye said, pinning Mary Anne with a shameless pleading look.

"A special group price," Teague echoed.

Mary Anne laughed. "Okay, okay. You two don't need to gang up on me. I'll take all four. I'll get my carriers from the truck."

"I will walk with you," Teague said.

"I'll get their shot records and other paperwork together," Baye said, jogging off toward Libby's table.

It was a difficult conversation as they walked to Mary Anne's truck since Teague couldn't, wouldn't explain why she was suddenly preparing for the rehoming of her animal family. She finally offered a small lie that attending her cousin's funeral had suddenly made her aware of the fragility of life.

❖

"First of all, nothing's going to happen to you," Mary Anne said. "Second, you're smart to think ahead, and I'd love to promise that I would take Asset back, but you have to remember why I gave him to you before. He constantly disrupted my classes with his loud braying because he wanted to get the attention of the kids who were there to learn to ride and show horses."

Teague sighed, accepted one of the two cat carriers Mary Anne took from her large SUV, and followed her back to the cathouse. "You are right. What about my llama? He rarely makes a sound."

Mary Anne shook her head. "I do know a sheep rancher who might take the llama to guard his flock. I can text you his information, if you like."

"Okay." Teague would rather hike barefoot through snow than ask a favor of a stranger. She wasn't good with people. She'd been friends with Mary Anne since she'd taken riding lessons from Mary Anne's mother as a teen. "Maybe."

"Look. Why don't you just set up a trust that would allow Connie to keep living there, managing the estate if something happened to you? She could take care of your animals until they live out their lives."

"It has been stipulated in the Maxwell wills through three generations that a Maxwell must own the estate. I'm bound by my parents' will to deed the estate to my next-closest blood relative in the event of my death."

They corralled the cats into the carriers, and Teague helped Mary Anne load them in her SUV. Mary Anne closed the rear hatch and reached out before stopping short of grabbing Teague's arm as Baye had earlier. She was aware Teague did not like to be touched.

"Teague, I've known you since we were teens, and I mean this in the kindest way. You obsess over things like a dog worrying a bone. Your cousin who died smoked, drank too much alcohol, and was overweight. You're a picture of health. You don't smoke, consume little alcohol—"

"It gives me a headache."

"—and Connie makes sure you eat right, even when you're deep into a project and ignoring your need to eat and sleep. You're still a young woman. Nothing's going to happen to you."

Teague wanted to blurt out that she'd just learned she'd likely inherited the Maxwell curse, but she was a scientist, and the term sounded silly when she voiced it aloud. So, she nodded. "Thank you. Good luck with the kittens."

"Come check out my new barn on Sunday. We can saddle a couple of horses and take a long trail ride. That should take your mind off that funeral."

A trail ride through the forest did sound inviting. "Yes. Maybe I will." Teague offered her a weak smile. "Go pay the ladies for your cats. I should go home to feed my minions."

Mary Anne laughed. "I think you can skip the crew still

hanging by the fence. They've eaten enough dog biscuits to call it dinner."

"You are probably right." Teague shook her head and waved a good-bye over her shoulder before climbing the fence to walk across the pasture to her home.

"Teague, hey. Wait up." Baye was sprinting toward her, so she turned back to wait for her at the fence.

"Yes?"

Baye slid to a stop and put her hand to her chest as she panted from her run. "Jesus, I'm out of shape." Her light brown curls fanned out in a wild halo and draped over her shoulders. Her eyes were a swirl of browns and greens Teague found intriguing.

"You did not have to run. I heard you and was waiting."

"Really?" Baye suddenly acted shy.

"I do not say things I do not mean."

Baye tilted her head, apparently trying to catch Teague's gaze, then gave up and spoke. "I just wanted to thank you for stopping by and helping me talk Mary Anne into an extra kitten."

Teague cocked her head. "We made a good team." She wasn't flirting. Her attempts to flatter or entice normally felt awkward and fell flat. So, she never flirted. She was simply reporting a fact based on the outcome of their cathouse encounter. Nevertheless, the observation seemed to please Baye.

"I was hoping I might meet the rest of your animals sometime. I mean, if you have time in your schedule for a curious neighbor."

This request pleased her, because she liked to show off her animals. "Of course. I expect to be home all week, so come over any time you are free."

Baye's shy smile broadened. "Great. That's great. Next week then?"

Teague felt strangely elated at the promise of seeing her again and returned her smile. "I will look forward to it."

❖

Libby shuffled the papers on her left and stabbed at the keypad of the calculator app on her phone. "I have good news and bad news."

Baye opened the oven a crack and peeked for the tenth time at the pizza heating inside it. She propped the pizza box next to the overflowing trash can, then grabbed a couple of sodas from the refrigerator and plopped them on the table next to Libby. Buoyed by the success of the adoption event, she flitted from one task to the next while ignoring the trash and sink full of dirty dishes. She was too hyped to sit down and chill. "Give me the good news. I don't want to hear any bad news today." She paused, greedy to know everything, then sat in a chair perpendicular to Libby's. "Forget I said that. I want to hear it all, but give me the good news first."

"The good news is that we adopted out eight dogs and twelve cats."

Baye jumped to her feet again. "Wow. That's really great." Seeing animals go off to their forever homes made her swell with happiness. It was truly her life's mission to see as many pets as possible find a loving home. "I cried when that couple chose Jocko." In fact, just the thought of his adoption tightened her throat and brought tears to her eyes even now. The brindle mutt had an unattractive overbite and only three legs, and was one of the first dogs they'd taken in. "I knew this was the best way to find homes for our babies."

Libby pinned her with a hard look. "But we're even deeper in the hole since the adoption fees collected were three hundred dollars less than the ice cream truck and the bounce house cost, plus buying fifteen pizzas to feed our volunteers before they left. Those high school kids are like a pack of starved wolves when they smell food."

Baye's joy deflated a bit. "Are you sure you added right?"

"Yes. I added everything correctly. Three times."

Baye brightened again. "Well, we'll have fewer mouths to

feed. I don't know how you can factor that in, but I bet that will at least let us break even for the month."

Libby shook her head. "I doubt it. Especially if you keep taking in new animals."

Baye flounced onto the sofa and glared at Libby. "What do you expect me to do? Let them roam the streets and starve?" Everybody was always raining on her good ideas.

Libby stood and glared back. "No, but many other rescues have more financial support than we do. Get a list of the local ones and give it to anyone looking to dump animals—at least until we can find a way to break even every month."

"They're probably full, too." She twisted to lie on the length of the sofa and scowled at the ceiling. "And what if the person turning in the animal decides that's too much trouble and just drives down the road and kicks it out of their car?"

"What if the animals we've taken in starve or go without medical treatment because we don't have money to take care of them properly? That's what happens to those animal hoarders. They start out trying to help homeless animals and end up overwhelmed with dogs and cats they can't afford to feed or give veterinary care."

Baye made a dismissive sound, still refusing to look at Libby. "We are not hoarders. And I'll pick up a few bartending jobs if I have to. Don't you worry about it."

"Look. We both work hard here, with only John to help, and he can't do everything. He's nearly eighty years old. You're the idea person, and I'm the financial person. We have to work together. Your idea for an adopt-a-thon was a good one, but you should have let me run the numbers before you went all crazy renting an ice cream truck and a bounce house. We could have figured out something less expensive. The kids hardly used the bounce house."

"Okay, okay. You're right, as usual."

"So, your idea for hosting birthday parties is a good one, but write down what you want to offer, and we'll price out the costs so we know we'll make money, not lose more."

Baye sat up, her mind reeling with possibilities that swept away her sulk. "I can do that. I've got so many ideas. I'll get to work on it right away."

"Good." Libby closed her laptop and put her papers neatly into a folder. Then she opened the dishwasher and began to load it with the dishes that covered every counter and were piled in the sink. "I don't want pizza again. I brought some of my homemade spaghetti and some garlic bread for dinner, but I can't cook or eat until I clean this messy kitchen."

"You're the best." Baye sprang from the sofa and engulfed her in a bear hug from behind. "I love your spaghetti."

"You're not getting any until you bag that trash and take it out. I swear, I don't know how you can stand living in all this mess."

"I've been busy planning today's adopt-a-thon."

"You're hopeless."

"You still love me."

Libby shook her head but smiled. "I don't know why, but I do."

Chapter Four

Baye rang the doorbell and stood nervously on the porch of the huge white mansion. She'd never been in a house so large and imposing. She couldn't imagine how only two people lived in a mansion that could easily house a dozen. She took a step back when the ferocious yapping of a small dog grew louder and the large door swung open.

"Quiet, Badger. Sit." The stern command quieted the small terrier mix. "Can I help you?" A gray-haired, older woman wearing a neat, casual cotton dress looked her over like she was an alien from Mars.

"Um, oh. Yes. I'm Baye, your neighbor." She pointed toward the rescue center, visible some distance away down the large hill. Her words tumbled out almost on top of each other as she hurried to explain. "I met Teague at our adopt-a-thon last week—we're an animal-rescue center—and she invited me to come meet her pets this week. Is she home?"

Clear, blue eyes appraised her again, but with a hint of humor. "You're not going to talk her into more animals, are you? I won't let you in if you're planning to do that. I can't keep up with the menagerie she has now."

"No, no. Not at all." Baye took a breath, glad she could pass this apparent requirement for entrance. "She wasn't looking to adopt any dogs or cats when she came by Saturday. She dropped by to talk to Mary Anne Beck when she recognized her truck parked at our place. I was curious when she told me about her unusual assortment of pets, and she invited me to come by to meet them."

"Well, that's a first. She doesn't usually invite people to her house." The woman stepped back and waved Baye inside. "I'm Connie, Teague's housekeeper."

"Thank you. We sort of connected over our love of animals," Baye said, taking in the marble floor and cathedral ceiling of the foyer. Badger sniffed her, then followed along.

"She's out in her lab as usual, working on something too complicated for me to understand—a thumbnail-sized battery that can power an entire space station or some other such nonsense," Connie said. "At least I don't have to put up with that noisy bird or thieving monkey when she's out there. They all go wherever she is. Well, except for Badger," she said, indicating the terrier. "He hangs out with me when he's not playing with Snow."

Was Snow another person? Perhaps Teague's partner or a relative? Wait. Didn't she say the big white dog's name was Snow?

Connie stopped and turned back to Baye. "I'm sorry. What did you say your name was?"

"Baye, spelled like it sounds, but with an *e* on the end. Baye Cobb."

"Baye. That's an unusual name."

"An old family name."

The woman held out her hand, and Baye took it in a quick handshake. "Pleased to meet you, Baye." She suddenly turned chatty as she led Baye through a pristine formal living room that looked as if the furniture had rarely, if ever, been sat upon. "I don't do any actual housekeeping. Teague says I'm a house manager, and I guess I am. Lord, this place is way too big for me to keep clean, but I arrange for a service to take care of that. I also arrange for any painters, plumbers, electricians, landscape services, and such when needed. This place is decades old, and old houses require constant upgrades and maintenance. Mostly, I cook for the two of us and do the laundry."

So, it was only the two of them. Baye peeked through partially open double doors they passed at a room filled to the ceiling with books. Two wingback chairs sat before a fireplace. It appeared recently used, if the plaid throw blanket draped over the arm of one chair was any indication. She could imagine sitting there to read a good book with a fire blazing in the hearth. The very thought warmed her, but she hurried to catch up to Connie, who was unlocking an ornate wrought-iron door that seemed very out of place in the middle of the house.

"This door stays locked to keep that monkey, the parrot, and their pig friend out of the main part of the house."

"The pig comes in the house?"

"She has better manners than the other two, but they're only allowed in here, and in Teague's rooms." Connie gestured to indicate the huge open-concept room with a kitchen at one end, separated by a large granite-topped island from a sitting area that appeared to be the actual living area. A big-screen television hung on the wall opposite an overstuffed, well-used sofa and reclining chair, separated by a parrot's perch from which colorful plastic toys and small, partially chewed wood blocks dangled. A half dozen knotted ropes hung from the exposed rafters of the vaulted ceiling, a massive cat tree stood by a window, and a baby's changing table was tucked unobtrusively in one corner of the room.

"Does Teague have a baby?" This was surprising since Baye's gaydar had pinged loudly when she met Teague at the adopt-a-thon. Not that lesbians couldn't have kids, but Teague didn't seem the type.

"That's for changing the monkey's diapers," Connie said when she saw Baye staring. "You can't house-train those devils. Can you believe that pig knows to go outside to do her business, but the monkey doesn't?" She checked to make sure the wrought-iron door locked back into place. "I don't change that rascal's diapers. That's all on Teague. And don't get me started on the things that loud-mouthed bird chews up."

Connie's complaining contained no venom, so Baye didn't take it too seriously as she trailed Connie through a large sunroom with two roomy cages, then out onto a plush lawn.

Connie pointed to a guest cottage on the other side of a pristine pool. "She and her gang of misfits are in there. We don't stand on formalities. Just go on in and announce yourself, loudly if she's absorbed in whatever she's doing. I swear you could burn that house down around her when she's in work mode."

Baye stared at the cottage, painted a stark white. Its green metal roof gleamed in the sun, and huge, tall windows flanked the door, which was painted to match the roof. Should she barge in if Teague was busy working? Maybe she should have called first. She turned to confirm that she'd be welcome, but Connie was already inside and closing the sunroom door. Badger hesitated, then pushed through a pet door to rejoin Connie.

Baye took a deep breath. Hopefully, she wouldn't interrupt anything important. She knocked quickly, then opened the door and stepped into chaos.

Strains of Motown coming from speakers built into the vaulted ceiling were nearly drowned out by the parrot's screams of "thief" and "thieving monkey," while the monkey held a piece of fruit in one hand and used his other hand and tail to swing among a series of ropes that dangled from the ceiling like in the big house. A feline the size of a bobcat climbed a four-by-four post bolted to the floor and wrapped in sisal rope, then leapt along a series of sturdy platforms attached to the wall. A massive white dog barked at the monkey, while Teague, her back to Baye and seemingly oblivious to the raucous animals, wrote in quick strokes a mathematical equation that was close to filling a five-feet-by-ten-feet whiteboard.

Then a pig, sprawled on a pet bed shaped like a couch, spied

Baye and filled the room with squeals that rivaled a heavy-metal concert, and everyone froze for a full two seconds.

Teague turned slowly to face her, then smiled broadly. "Hello." She had to shout over the pig's renewed squeals. "Quiet, Flower."

Baye shifted her feet nervously. "I hope I'm not interrupting your work," she shouted back since Flower had ignored Teague's command for quiet.

"I am sorry. She is a more enthusiastic watchdog than Snow is." Teague gestured to the huge dog. "Her eyesight is poor, and she does not recognize your scent." She was at Baye's side in three long strides. "If you do not mind...Flower, come here." Teague stooped to Flower's level and indicated for Baye to do the same. "Let her sniff you. She does not bite. She likes to be scratched behind her ears."

Flower lumbered forward and thoroughly sniffed Baye's shoes and up her leg. Her sprig of a tail swished back and forth, and then she stepped back and pinned Baye with her dark, beady eyes. Baye held out her hand for Flower to sniff, her nose soft but not damp, as she expected. "Hey, Flower. I'm a friend of your mom." She cautiously scratched behind one ear, and Flower's happy little grunts seemed to indicate she appreciated the move and approved her presence.

"See? Baye is a friend."

"Pretty, pretty," Mac said, fluffing his feathers and turning his head this way and that for a better look. "Pretty lady."

"Flower is very smart. People underestimate pigs all the time. I would approximate her intelligence to be the same as a six-year-old child. She loves painting and watching cartoons."

Baye straightened. "She paints and watches television?"

"Well, I try to limit her television-watching and encourage her to take walks with some of the rest of us. She loves to eat, and even the smaller potbellied pigs can grow huge if they are fed too much. It is not good for her heart, just like being obese would negatively impact a person's health."

"Wow. All I know about pigs is that they like to roll in mud and pig pens stink."

Teague shook her head. "Pigs can be taught to relieve themselves outdoors, just like a dog. Pig farms stink because they are overcrowded and without proper means to keep them clean. Pigs do like to wallow in mud, but they do it because they cannot sweat. The mud keeps them cool and protected from insects."

"I had no idea." Teague's knowledge of her animals fascinated her. "Will you introduce me to the rest?"

Teague gestured to the dog, who then came to nuzzle Baye's hand. "This is Snow, obviously named for his heavy white coat. He's a Great Pyrenees mix. Snow's previous owner lived in an apartment, which was totally unsuitable for such a huge, active animal, so he came to live with me. He hangs out and sleeps inside during the day, but he stays out with the small herd of goats and sheep at night."

"You kick him out at night?"

Teague raised her eyebrows. "He is a working breed and needs a job to be happy. He loves watching over the other animals and has chased off more than one coyote after a lamb, or a fox sniffing around the chickens."

"Who watches over them during the day?"

"Lucky the llama covers the day shift. He sometimes rests in the barn after Snow takes over the guard duties at dark."

"Well, that works out well for all, I guess."

"They worked it out between themselves, so I went along with it." Teague bent to let the macaw climb onto her arm and walked him over to place him on a perch with cups on either end to hold water and food. "This is Mac the macaw. Say hello to Baye, Mac."

Mac turned his head this way and that before he spoke. "Hello, Pretty."

"No. Her name is Baye."

"Pretty."

"Hello, Mac," Baye said, offering her hand to him. He carefully clasped her finger in his beak, and she giggled when he ran his small tongue over her skin. "He's beautiful, but that's a really big beak."

"He will be careful because he likes you. He does not care for men, and his bite can do a bit of damage. He is okay with Bruce, who helps me clean up after the animals, but it took a while for Mac to trust him. I think a man must have abused him before I rescued him from a roadside zoo. His feathers were in terrible shape from mites, and the outdoor cage he was kept in was filthy."

Mac had moved from tasting Baye's skin to tonguing the texture of her T-shirt, and then examining her hair. Teague stopped him when he tried to climb onto her shoulder. "Whoa, there. Baye might not appreciate it if you poop on her shirt."

"Pretty," Mac said, spreading his huge wings, then settling back onto his perch to bob his head and chant a much more interesting word. "Poop. Poop. Monkey poop. Monkey poop."

Baye laughed. "I'm guessing he doesn't get along with the monkey."

Teague clapped her hands softly, and the capuchin monkey watching them from overhead dropped into her arms. "This is Captain, Cappie for short. He and Mac have a love-hate relationship. Cappie is constantly stealing food from Mac, but Mac also steals from him and beats him up with his wings. I think it is more of a game they play than any real aggression, because neither tries to bite nor injure the other. I sometimes catch them grooming each other."

"That would be a great YouTube video."

Teague shrugged as Cappie settled on her shoulder, wrapping his tail around her neck and vocalizing in little squeaks. He stared at her curiously but clung to Teague. "I do not have time for social media. It is a distraction from my work, and I prefer to spend my free time with my animals."

The gigantic cat leapt down to the floor, sniffed at Baye's jeans, and began to rub his face against her leg. "Well, hello," she said, bending to pet him.

"That is Leo. He is a Maine coon cat I inherited when one of my cousins died. They are a large and friendly breed."

"He's sweet." Baye pointed to the whiteboard half covered with the equation Teague was writing when she arrived. "What kind of work do you do?"

Teague shrugged again. Baye was beginning to realize she tended to do that when she didn't like the subject or wasn't sure how to respond. "My doctorate is in physics, but I also have degrees in mechanical and biomedical engineering. Physics is mostly proving a lot of theories that are the building blocks of practical applications. I enjoy solving engineering problems the most, but often go back to physics to lay the groundwork to solve those problems."

"So, do you own a company or work for somebody like NASA?"

"I have done work for NASA, but also for companies like General Motors, IBM, and the government. It is strictly contract work. I will never limit myself by working for one company."

Baye stared at the whiteboard in awe. "Can you explain what you're working on now, or is it top secret?"

Teague studied the equation she'd been writing. "I am between contracts now. This is my own project. There is always a need for smaller, more powerful, longer-lasting batteries. I am looking to develop a battery the size of a pinhead that can power an airplane across the Atlantic, an electric car thousands of miles, or a submarine. Ultimately, however, I would like to develop a completely new source of energy. We must do that before fossil fuels destroy our environment."

"Wow. How do you get these contracts? I'd be afraid I wouldn't get a new one when I needed to pay bills."

"I hold several patents that bring in millions every year, and my success with past contracts has earned me a reputation that attracts new work. I turn down probably fifty contracts for every one that I accept."

"Why would you do that?" Baye would have been put off by what many would deem to be bragging, but she realized Teague was simply giving her the information she requested.

The shrug again. "Mostly because the problem they want me to solve is not much of a challenge. Any of their engineers could find the answer if they just stepped back and looked at the wider picture. Also, I refuse any military contracts that involve weaponry, but I will consider anything that would improve the safety or comfort of the soldiers and sailors serving."

"So, what was the last contract you completed?"

"To put it simply, NASA had a gyroscope problem in the mechanical arms on space shuttles. They needed precision control of the arms in a weightless environment, and the mechanics had stumped their engineers. I came up with a solution."

"Wow."

Teague smiled. "It was one of my more challenging contracts. I thoroughly enjoyed it."

"So, you like solving puzzles others can't."

"I do not see it as besting NASA's top engineers, but as a test of my ability to resolve the problem." She absently scratched Cappie, who still perched on her shoulder. "It is time for our daily walk. Would you like to join us?"

This woman was way out of her league, but Baye couldn't resist the chance to spend more time with the beautiful, fascinating Teague. "I'd love to."

❖

"Come on, Flower." Teague literally dangled a carrot to entice the pig to follow her into the yard. "Snow, stay and rest."

The big dog returned inside, jumped onto the dog couch Flower had abandoned, and curled up with a sigh. Still, they were quite a parade with her and Baye in the lead, Cappie on Teague's shoulder, Leo patrolling around them, Flower grunting at their heels, and Mac walking awkwardly last and occasionally flying short distances to catch up.

"Aren't you afraid your monkey—"

"Cappie." Teague wanted her to get to know the animals before she proposed the plan she'd decided on last night.

Baye nodded. "Aren't you afraid Cappie will hop off your shoulder and disappear into the trees? Or that Mac will fly off?"

A lush, expansive lawn stretched down the hill to a traditional red barn, and, beyond that, a three-acre, spring-fed pond was ringed on three sides with a forest of hardwoods.

"An osprey pair nests on the other side of the pond for a while each year, and Cappie is too scared of them to leave his perch on my shoulder. Mac's flight wings are clipped, so he cannot gain enough altitude to fly very far. He will likely turn back before we get halfway to the barn."

Baye stopped, and they both checked on Mac's progress. Sure enough, the macaw was already making his way back to the cottage. He paused at the door to the cottage, then peered up at the sky. "Danger, danger, Will Robinson," he croaked.

The shadow of an osprey passed over, and Mac hopped the rest of the way into the cottage. Cappie burrowed into Teague's dark, shoulder-length hair, and she reached up to reassure him. Leo was oblivious, intent on catching a successfully elusive butterfly.

"Have the ospreys ever tried to attack Mac?"

"I think it was more of a closer-look kind of thing because their preferred diet is fish, and I keep the pond stocked for them. But when one of them swooped low once, Flower ran squealing to protect Mac. The osprey wisely decided against tangling with a two-hundred-pound pig."

"Really? A guard pig?"

"Well, Snow was sleeping inside, and Lucky was with the sheep and goats." It made perfect sense to Teague that Flower would protect her friend, but Baye seemed to find it surprising.

"Amazing." Baye paused to let Flower catch up, then bent to give her a vigorous back-scratching. Flower lifted her nose, much like a dog, and issued pleased little grunts. "What a good piggy!" After a moment, she straightened, and they resumed their trek to the barn.

A small flock of chickens scurried out to meet them, and several Canada geese honked and ran toward them from the pond.

The laugh bubbling up from Baye warmed Teague's chest. Was she smiling again? It wasn't that she didn't smile much, but Baye's joyful response to everything had Teague smiling much more than usual.

"Look at you," Baye cooed to the hens surrounding them. "They're beautiful. I love the ones with feathers on their feet."

Pleased, Teague picked up a fat brown hen and stroked her. The hen made low clucking sounds. "This is Miss Hennie. She is the leader of the flock."

"Not the rooster?" Baye pointed to the lone rooster that was scratching and pecking at the ground a little distance away.

"He is old and mostly just hangs around without bothering the hens. He is past his breeding days, but he will chase Leo because he mistakenly sees him as a threat. Do you want to pet her?" she asked when Baye returned her attention to Miss Hennie. To her surprise, Baye reached out to take the hen from her rather than simply stroke her. She handed Miss Hennie over, showing her how to hold her comfortably and securely.

"Are they all this tame?"

"Some do not care for being picked up or petted, but I raised Miss Hennie from a chick and handled her often so that she enjoys it." She watched Miss Hennie settle against Baye's chest and resume her low clucking. "Did you know that a hen can transition to become a rooster?"

Baye looked up, her hazel eyes wide and gray-green in the sunlight. "There are trans chickens?"

"Yes. It is a rare genetic condition, but if a hen's only functioning ovary is damaged, the non-functioning ovary can develop into a structure known as an avo-testis, which produces male hormones that cause her to grow male plumage. They are not capable of fertilizing eggs, but it does not keep them from acting like a rooster." Teague liked passing along knowledge and was pleased that Baye seemed interested instead of bored with her mini-lectures.

Baye stroked Miss Hennie. "I knew that with some animal species, same-sexes might pair off, but I had no idea there were also trans animals." She looked up at Teague. "We humans are not as unique as we think, are we?" she said softly.

Teague briefly met her gaze. "No. We are not."

Baye gently placed Miss Hennie down so she could rejoin her flock, and they stepped into the barn, dimly lighted by the sun shining in from the large rollback doors at either end. Teague opened a door to their immediate right to reveal a room packed with various bags of feed for the different animals. She filled a small cloth bag with alfalfa cubes, then scooped out a handful of cracked corn and tossed it into the barn's hallway. The chickens scrambled to gobble it up.

"Is that what you feed them? Corn?"

"No. That is an occasional treat. A more balanced chicken feed goes in their feeders in the morning and at night."

The door opposite the feed room opened, and a young man stepped out. "Hey, Teague. I thought I heard you out here."

"Bruce, this is my neighbor, Baye. I am giving her a small tour of the estate. She and her cousin own the pet rescue next door."

He held out his hand to Baye. "Nice to meet you. We'd been wondering about all the construction going on there for a while. Then I noticed your sign went up a few months ago. I love the name…Heavy Petting."

Baye shook his offered hand. "Thanks. It was my idea but took some convincing to get my cousin to go along with it. She was afraid people would drive by and think it was a massage parlor."

Bruce laughed. "Good thing that you added 'pet rescue' in smaller letters. But don't let me interrupt your tour." He stepped back so Baye could see the room behind him. Several saddles and a dozen halters with lead ropes attached hung on the wall opposite a battered desk. Cappie immediately jumped from Teague's shoulder to climb among the halters and lead ropes. "This is the office. I'm a third-year veterinary student at State College, so I'm normally only here before classes, then in the early evening after classes to feed and clean pens."

"Coming up on exam week?" Teague asked.

"You know it." Bruce turned to Baye. "Teague lets me study in the barn office because my roommates are too rowdy and the library too distracting as people come and go. There's nothing to divert my attention but an occasional visit from one of the curious animals. I don't usually close the door, but Abigail's twins keep coming in and trying to snatch my notes and eat them."

As if summoned, the two kid goats tried to clamor past Baye and Teague, who each caught one before they could reach the tasty papers on the desk.

"We will leave you to it and get the goats out of your hair," Teague said, tucking the small kid under one arm and patting her shoulder with her free hand. "Come on, Cappie. No. Leave Bruce's pencil here." She took the pencil from her pilfering monkey when he returned to her shoulder and handed it back to Bruce. "Sorry. He has chewed off the eraser."

"There's more in the desk," Bruce said, smiling as he returned to his studies. Teague closed his door, and they set the kids down to rejoin their mother.

"Do you ride? I saw the saddles and stuff," Baye said.

"I used to show in hunter classes but do not have the time now. I still ride occasionally with Mary Anne."

The rest of the barn was sectioned off into five large stalls filled with wood chips, while a sixth had been converted into a chicken coop.

Teague watched as Baye peeked into each one, stopping

at the last stall on the right. She turned to Teague, wonder illuminating her features. The sun was much lower now, its rays highlighting the blond streaks in the light brown curls that draped over Baye's shoulders. Beautiful. She mentally shook herself when she realized Baye was speaking to her. "Sorry?"

"The cat…Leo is licking those big rabbits," she said.

Teague stepped up beside her, maybe a little too close, and cleared her throat, which tightened as she inhaled Baye's lavender scent. "Um, yes. I am never sure if he is grooming the rabbits or tasting them, but he has never hurt either."

"Do all the animals sleep in the barn at night?"

"Only in rainy or very cold weather. The hens do come in to roost each night, and Bruce or I lock them up to keep them safe in case a fox tries to creep into the barn. Then I let them out around mid-morning after most have finished laying eggs. The rabbits generally are nocturnal animals and wander the yard at night. They are Flemish Giants, large enough to defend themselves against most danger, and Snow is on guard against big predators like coyotes. Lucky, the llama, and Asset, my donkey, come in some nights, but they usually prefer to stay out on nice ones. The barn and stalls are always open to give them a choice unless a storm is coming and I want them tucked safely inside."

They left the barn and walked toward the wood fence that enclosed the pond and the large pasture that separated their homes.

"This is like a real farm, isn't it? We're only set up for dogs and cats at the rescue, but I wouldn't mind taking some pigs or chickens, too."

"Well, this would only be a real farm if the animals were used for food production. These are pets. I bought the sheep, all ewes, because they were destined for the butcher since they were too old to breed. The hens are the only food producers. They lay eggs pretty much year-round. Their peak production is during the summer, and I pass along what I can't eat to the local food bank."

She smiled at Baye. "So, do not buy eggs this summer. When you run out, just pop over and get a fresh dozen from me or Connie."

"I'll do that." Baye fell quiet as they walked.

After a while, Teague spoke. "I guess you stay pretty busy with the day-to-day business of running a rescue."

Baye nodded but stared at the ground. "My grandmother left a trust that pays for John, and he lives in a cottage on the property. Grams called him her gardener, but he's much more than that. He also our handyman and kennel cleaner. He doesn't have any close family. He's in exceptionally good health, but he's approaching eighty and not physically able to do everything. I'm trying to figure out how to pull in more donations so we can hire some help for the kennels."

Teague's ears pricked up at this news. It could work in her favor. "What if—" Asset's raucous brays drowned any hope of conversation as he ran across the pasture, obviously having just spotted them. Lucky strolled sedately behind him. Teague opened the small bag of alfalfa cubes she'd hooked onto her belt, handing several cubes to Baye and one to Cappie. She was pleased that Baye seemed familiar with the treat and held one out to Asset as he reached the fence.

"Hello, handsome," Baye said to Asset, scratching his chin. She laughed when Cappie jumped from Teague's shoulder to the board fence and held out a cube to Asset. When the donkey took it, Cappie jumped from the fence to cling to Asset's neck, then sat on his back and began grooming his spiky mane. Baye's delighted laughter made Teague smile again.

"They are great friends," she said. "I occasionally take walks through the woods beyond the pond, and several of the animals like to follow. Cappie feels safe with Asset and will ride on his back during those walks."

"What happened to Asset's ear?"

"A roaming pack of dogs attacked and nearly killed him when he was a yearling. Several other donkeys in the field chased them off, but not before the dogs chewed his ear so badly it had to be amputated. His owner said he could not afford the vet bill for an amputation and told the vet to put him down. I paid for the operation in exchange for ownership. He boarded at Mary Anne's for a while to be with other equines, but his friendly nature distracted her riding students. He does not appear to mind that his friends here are not horses."

Baye—brown, green, and gray swirling in her eyes as she faced the sun—turned to gaze at Teague. "All of your animals have a story, don't they?"

"They are all rescued from some tragic situation, except for Leo the cat, whose owner died. I am sure a rescue group would get multiple applications from potential adopters, but I promised my cousin I would take care of him."

Lucky finally arrived and took several of the alfalfa treats from Teague but refused the one Baye held out for him.

"Llamas can be very suspicious, distrustful animals. He will not take food from you or let you pet him because he does not know you."

"How did you get him to like you?"

"Llamas, as well as most equines, are very curious. I just sat in the middle of their pasture, reading a book, and after a short time, Lucky was looking over my shoulder, then sniffing my book. So, I laid a couple of cubes on the book, and she began swiping them. Soon, she was taking them from my hand."

"I didn't know that about llamas…Actually, I don't know much at all about them. I do know about horses but didn't realize they were so curious."

When Teague gestured to the pond in silent invitation, Baye nodded and followed. Flower was wallowing in a muddy puddle on the bank, and two Canada geese were paddling toward them with five goslings trailing in their wake. Teague pulled a sandwich-sized plastic bag from her pocket and poured seeds from it into her hand, then tossed it across the water. The geese hungrily gobbled up the seeds floating around them.

"What are you feeding them?"

"Wheat. It is part of their natural diet. A lot of people think they are looking for insects when they peck away at a lawn, but they are eating the grass. They enjoy a variety of land and water plants and grains, and they will browse a wheat field after it has been harvested to pick up seeds that were left behind." She held out the bag. "Do you want to throw them some?" She poured the rest of the wheat kernels into Baye's cupped hand, which she unnecessarily held in her own as she emptied the bag. Her slightly larger hand seemed coarse, and her nails unpainted, compared to Baye's slender fingers and manicured nails.

The watchful adults swam as close to them as they seemed to think safe, eyeing Cappie, who was chattering at them from his perch on her shoulder, and Flower, who was grunting happily in her mud bath. Still, they again gobbled up the wheat grain Baye cast across the water near them.

"They're so beautiful." Baye tilted her head thoughtfully. "Isn't it amazing how nature creates such detailed markings, then duplicates those markings on each generation after?"

"Genetics are a mystery that scientists are only beginning to unlock." Teague shook her head. "Do not get me started. I could discuss the subject for days. I believe genes could be at the root of future scientific advancements, even areas we now see as unrelated to genetics." She'd solved many problems that stumped other scientists and engineers simply because they were too focused and failed to consider a broader view of possibilities.

Baye laughed suddenly and pointed to Flower, who had emerged from her mud pit and plunged into the pond to swim toward the geese, scattering them. "I've never seen a pig swim before!"

"Flower enjoys swimming. After she has had a bath, I sometimes let her in the pool at the house. She will swim laps with me, which helps keep her fit and lean."

Teague watched Flower swim after the geese but could feel Baye's gaze on her and wished she was wearing something better than her faded T-shirt, jeans, and worn leather flip-flops. But Baye had caught her off-guard. She normally hated unannounced intrusions and was surprised that Baye's did not bother her. In fact, it pleased her. She mentally shook herself. Back to business. "I have a proposal for you."

Baye's wide smile seemed to brighten the already sunny day. "Really? We just met, and you're proposing already? We haven't even kissed yet."

"What? No." Heat rose from her chest to her cheeks as she whirled to face Baye, even though she couldn't meet her gaze. The strange communication horrified her. "Of course not. That would hardly be proper."

Baye clasped Teague's forearm. "I was kidding." Her laughter bubbled up even though she put her free hand to her mouth to stifle it. "You should see the panic on your face." She lowered her hand and mimicked Teague, but in a poor imitation of a British accent. "That would hardly be proper." She giggled again. "Are you British? You speak so properly sometimes that it reminds me of the Brits' stiff upper lip."

"I have no accent. Just because I use proper English does not mean I am British." She pulled her arm from Baye's grasp and glowered at her. Her lack of social skills was a sore nerve. "Most educated people speak proper English."

Baye took several steps back, her smile faltering. "Whoa. I was not disrespecting you."

Baye had hit on one of Teague's biggest pet peeves. "You were not *showing* disrespect. It is a noun, not a verb." Teague growled the correction. It was one of a handful of words she detested.

Baye's smile vanished, and she returned Teague's scowl. "It's in the dictionary."

"I refuse to acknowledge what the people we call scholars today add to the dictionary. They probably learned their language skills by wasting time on social media and playing video games.

Those younger generations can concentrate on video games for hours but cannot focus enough to earn a college degree."

Baye's face was growing redder by the second. "Maybe I don't have a wall full of college degrees like you, but that doesn't mean I'm stupid or undereducated." She crossed her arms over her chest. "I thought we might become friends. My mistake. I know you're really smart, but I don't need another person in my life who looks down on me." She whirled around and headed across the pasture toward her property.

Teague stared after her, the shock of Baye's sudden departure warring with Teague's indignation. "Fuck." People always made fun of her quirks. Her lack of eye contact and stilted manner of speech, refusing to use contractions, were two of the first things they usually noticed. That was why she preferred the company of her animals.

Chapter Five

"What a high-and-mighty bitch." Baye stormed into the farmhouse. "I don't care how sexy she is, I can see now why she doesn't have friends and lives like a recluse."

"Who has you so worked up?"

She jumped and slapped her hand over her chest. She was sure her heart missed a few beats. She hadn't noticed Libby seated at the dining room table with the month's bills and receipts spread around her laptop. "Holy crap. You nearly made me have a heart attack."

Libby snorted, her gaze never leaving the spreadsheet she was updating. "Considering all the crazy things you did when we were growing up and all the drugs you've smoked or ingested during your short lifetime, I seriously doubt you'll get a heart attack from being surprised." She looked up at Baye. "I'll ask again—who has you so worked up?"

"Teague."

"Who?"

"The neighbor who came to the adopt-a-thon."

"Ah. Tall, dark, and mysterious."

"More like stuck-up, condescending, and rude."

"She seemed nice on Saturday."

She took a breath…or two. "She can be, but watch out for her to explode into a raging snob." She waved her arms about as she ranted. "She was proposing to me one minute, and then it was like I stepped on a land mine a second later. She started ranting about uneducated people and misuse of the English language."

Libby's eyebrows shot up. "She proposed to you? I thought Saturday was the first time you'd met."

She shook her head. "Yes…no. Argh. Saturday *was* the first time we met. This afternoon, she said she had a proposal for me, and I teased her that it was too soon since she hadn't even kissed me yet. I meant it as a teasing invitation to kiss me."

"You wanted her to kiss you?"

Baye made a dismissive sound. "Who wouldn't? You've seen her. She's walking, talking sex on a stick."

"She's tall for a woman, but I'll admit she is attractive in a lesbian sort of way." Libby was decidedly heterosexual but had no problem with Baye's preference for women.

Baye hesitated but didn't want to get into a discussion about what "lesbian sort of way" meant. "Instead of kissing me, she got all flustered and said a proposal after knowing each other such a short time—and I quote—'would hardly be proper.' Then I made small joke about her sort of formal way of speaking, hoping she would relax again."

"But she didn't?"

"She turned into an attack dog—not literally—and said educated people knew how to speak proper English. I said I didn't mean to disrespect her, and she corrected my grammar."

"Oh, no. I know how much you hate that."

She drew herself up to stand stiff and straight with her nose tilted upward. "Disrespect is a noun, not a verb," she said in a snobby imitation of Teague.

"What did you say?"

"I told her that just because I didn't have a college degree and she had"—Baye searched her memory of the afternoon—"like four advanced degrees, didn't mean I was uneducated."

"Wow. She hit all your sore spots, didn't she?"

"She made my blood boil. I had to get away before I lost

it and slapped her, so I left her by the pond and took a shortcut through the pasture to come home."

"Crap. I guess hoping for a large donation, any donation from her, is out of the question."

"We don't need her money."

"Yes, we do."

Baye was already pissed off and didn't need to pick a second fight in the same day, so she stormed into the kitchen and slammed cabinet doors under the pretense of searching for food. Banging the doors helped bleed off the anger that gripped her.

Libby left her work and stood in the kitchen's doorway. "Didn't you drive over there?" She raised her voice to be heard over the commotion.

Baye halted her tantrum and dropped her chin to the chest. Her SUV was indeed still parked in front of the Maxwell mansion. "Shit."

❖

Teague bypassed the cottage and stomped her way to the house, pausing only to hose off Flower, who was following her. Mac was dining in his sunroom cage, so she placed Cappie in his equally large cage next to it and closed the doors on both. She wasn't ready for them to distract her from her anger. Sensitive to her moods, Cappie disappeared into his nest—a small cat bed on a platform situated high in the nine-feet-tall cage. His obvious move to hide checked her temper a little. She retrieved a banana from the kitchen and placed half of it on his food tray, relieved to see him scamper down, grab it, then take it back to his nest to enjoy the treat. She gave the other half to Mac, who mumbled "treat" as he peeled, then began to eat the fruit.

Then she returned to the kitchen for a glass of water. She drank little else, spurning sodas and energy drinks, and allowing herself one glass of sugary sweet tea a day unless she was pulling an all-nighter to work and needed the energy boost. It was one of the many rules she made for herself. Although she couldn't control her bouts of inspiration that might keep her at the whiteboard or her computer for days or cause her to rise in the middle of the night to work out an elusive solution to a problem, rules helped her stay in control of everything else.

"Where's your friend?"

"I do not have friends."

"I'm talking about the lovely young lady I sent to the cottage."

"She left." Teague ignored Connie's raised eyebrow.

Connie pointed to a plate filled with crackers, small squares of ham and cheese, and peanut-butter-and-banana sandwiches cut into quarters with the crust trimmed off. "That's a shame. I made some snacks for both of you." She placed a bowl of melon and pineapple cubes next to it. "I saw you two at the fence, feeding the donkey. I was surprised you left your work to show her around, but you seemed to be enjoying yourselves."

"We are not friends. She does not speak proper English." She helped herself to several of the sandwich squares. *Mmm. Sweet.* It was mid-afternoon and she hadn't had lunch yet. She speared a pineapple cube with a cocktail toothpick and popped it into her mouth. *Juicy.* Connie had been making these plates for her since she was a child and never forgot her toothpick quirk—no regular toothpicks or even a fork.

"Ah. I'm guessing she must have said something about how you talk."

Teague sometimes hated that Connie knew her triggers so well. "She said she was not disrespecting me. Disrespect is a noun, not a verb."

Connie extracted her phone from her jeans and tapped on the screen for several seconds. "Actually, it has been recognized as a verb since the sixteenth century and used as one through much of the seventeenth century. Using it as a verb sort of died out during the eighteenth century, when speech became wordy and more formal, but the usage was revived by the millennial generation." Connie knew how to check Teague's temper.

"You cannot believe everything you read on the internet."

Connie stepped closer and, grasping Teague's forearm, gave it a squeeze. She was one of few people she let touch her affectionately. "And you find it very hard to admit when you are wrong."

She pretended to be intent on choosing what she would eat next from the plate. "I am rarely wrong."

Connie grasped Teague's chin and lifted it, forcing her to briefly meet her gaze. "Perhaps you were wrong in this situation?"

"Maybe partly wrong?" Teague gently pulled her chin free and stuffed another sandwich square into her mouth.

"This isn't a negotiation, Teague. You were wrong and should apologize to her."

"She's gone, and I do not think she'll answer the door if I go to her house."

"Are you sure she left? I've been here in the kitchen the whole time and haven't seen her come back through to her car."

"She drove over?"

"Yes. Why would you think otherwise?"

"Because she stormed off across the pasture to return to her own house." Her voice rose with her effort to hold on to her anger and indignation.

"Just because you—inaccurately, I'll remind you—corrected her speech?"

"She remarked on my language first." Teague knew she sounded like a petulant child, but she had to defend herself. Didn't she? She threw her hands up. "Then she went on some rant about not having college degrees does not mean you are uneducated."

"You said she was uneducated?"

She scowled at Connie. She could be so damned insightful, a skill that eluded Teague. "Of course not. I simply said that educated people know how to speak correct English."

"So, you basically called her uneducated."

"I was speaking in a general sense. I know nothing about her education. Why would I remark about her specifically?"

"Maybe she didn't go to college. A lot of successful people don't. It sounds like it's a sensitive issue for her. Think about how angry you get when people make insensitive remarks about you."

The truth of the remark deflated the last of her annoyance. "I did not intend to insult her."

Connie patted her hand. "I know, honey. You should explain that to her. Maybe you should explain your struggle with sensitivity issues."

"That would have her locking her door to keep me out."

"I have a feeling you're wrong about that, too. Go talk to her. She took the first step toward friendship by coming over here. Now it's your turn. Her car is probably still parked out front. Drive next door and offer her a ride back here to retrieve it."

She considered this suggestion. It was a valid excuse for going over there. "Okay." She stood to go to the garage.

"Teague?"

She turned back to Connie. "Yes?"

"Apologize first so she'll be more amenable to accept your offer to drive her back here."

"Right. Apologize first."

❖

Teague studied the vehicles in the expansive garage. She loved mechanical things. Which should she take? The Jeep Cherokee, her usual mode of transportation, or the Mustang convertible? She started to grab the keys to the Mustang. That should rid Baye of the notion that she was too stiff and formal. Then she spotted the motorcycle parked at the far end. Perfect.

CHAPTER SIX

Baye peeked through the front window at the roar of an engine stopping in front of the farmhouse. A tall, helmeted figure killed the motor and engaged the kickstand, then dismounted the flashy red motorcycle. She waited while the person pulled off her helmet and shook out her dark hair. Teague. What the hell? She opened the front door and stepped onto the porch.

"Is that yours?" she asked without preamble.

"Hello again. Yes, it is mine. It is a 2023 Ducati SuperSport 950, delivered just last week." Teague smiled at her.

This was so weird. Her neighbor was like a light switch—rude, friendly, rude, friendly. The friendly person she first met stood before her.

"Would you like to go for a ride?"

"Just like that?" Baye frowned. "An hour ago, you were yelling and insulting me. Why should I go with you now?"

Teague mumbled something to herself and shuffled her feet for a moment. "I came to apologize. You did not misuse the English language, as I have since learned." She shifted the helmet in her arms before clearing her throat. "I never meant to insult your intelligence or your educational background, which I know nothing about."

Baye didn't respond. She'd been misunderstood and criticized her entire life, and Teague's earlier rush to judgment had bruised her deeply.

Teague lifted a shoulder in her familiar shrug and stared at her feet. "I hang out with my animals because I am not very good with people. I…I have a disability that has made me the subject of ridicule since I was a child. You touched on a sore spot when you teased me about my pattern of speech." She finally met Baye's gaze again. "If you will accept my apology, I would like to offer you a ride back to my estate so you can retrieve your car."

This super-smart woman had a disability? Teague's speech and lack of eye contact made sense now. Baye's resolve to hold on to her grudge melted away. She didn't have a lot of friends either because they couldn't understand or grew tired of dealing with her attention-deficit/hyperactivity disorder. "I accept your apology and offer mine to you. I overreacted when you corrected my grammar." How much should she say? "I've been criticized a lot because I haven't lived up to my family's expectations, so my lack of a college degree is a sore spot for me. I would like if we became friends as well as neighbors."

Teague briefly met her eyes, then looked away. "I expect if we become friends, we will stumble onto other sensitive subjects," she said.

Baye nodded. "*As* we become friends and get to know each other better, we'll have fewer and fewer explosions like today."

Teague's smile was small, but it was a smile. "Your use of fewer rather than less is perfect. Most people get that wrong." It was her best effort at a compliment to ease the tension.

She laughed. "If correct usage gets you to smile, I'll have to think of another." Maybe next time the reward could be a kiss.

Teague's cheeks pinked, and she handed over the extra helmet that had been strapped to the Ducati. "You have to wear a helmet. It is a law in this state."

"Normally, I wouldn't care about breaking a law for the short trip to your place, but I have an idea that might be another sore spot for you."

Teague frowned. "You should always obey the rules, Baye."

"And we will," she said, snugging the helmet onto her head

and flipping the face shield up, happy to see Teague's smile had reappeared. Yay. Explosion averted.

❖

They rolled to a gentle stop in front of the mansion, and Baye climbed down from where she was literally lying on Teague's back. This Ducati wasn't designed for comfortably carrying passengers. But damn! She would ride on it all day long just to lie on that long back and feel Teague's heartbeat speed up when she wrapped her arms around Teague's lean torso. She bent to pull her helmet off and swing her head back and forth a few times to fluff her long, curly locks after their confinement. "That was so much fun." She straightened to find Teague, helmet off, staring at her before glancing away. "Could we ride some more?"

Teague fidgeted with the strap on her helmet in her lap, but she didn't dismount from the bike, or answer.

"I'm sorry," Baye said, backtracking because of Teague's hesitation. "I've disrupted your day enough. You probably need to get back to work."

Teague blinked. "I am always working on a problem or idea in the back of my mind, but I am also good at multitasking, so it never keeps me from doing other things."

"You can work on one of those long equations like the one on your whiteboard, then remember all of it later to write it down?"

"It is part of my disability."

"Disability? I would call that a gift. I wish I could do that. Hell, I can't seem to focus on one thing for very long, much less multitask."

Teague cocked her head. "You were doing multiple things at the adopt-a-thon."

"Which I promptly forgot when you arrived and never finished."

"When I arrived?"

"Yes." Baye decided to take a chance and softened her voice.

"How could I focus on anything else when you showed up with your handsome face and intense eyes?"

Teague fiddled with the chin strap on the helmet again, and Baye waited to give her time to digest her flirtation. Teague cleared her throat. "You are very pretty."

Baye smiled at Teague's matter-of-fact tone. "So, can we ride a little longer on your motorcycle? If we go to the highway, we can go faster."

"You cannot be comfortable riding behind me. This Ducati was not designed to carry two people on a long trip."

"I wasn't uncomfortable. Was I too heavy, leaning on your back like that?"

"Not at all." Teague's face flushed red, and she lowered her voice as though she were speaking to herself rather than Baye. "I could feel your heart beating."

"Then we can ride some more?" She put her hands together as though praying or begging. "Please."

"Helmets back on," Teague ordered, and started the bike's engine again.

Baye eagerly complied and climbed on. She couldn't see Teague's expression with their helmets on, but she did feel her heart beating faster and stronger when she curled against her back and wrapped her arms around her.

Teague drove carefully at first, but then she gunned the throttle after they turned onto the nearby two-way blacktop.

"Woo-hoo," Baye shouted. The wind rushing around them, the vibration of the powerful engine, and the heat of Teague's body against hers were intoxicating.

They stayed within ten miles of the speed limit, but seventy miles per hour was much more thrilling than thirty. After they rode aimlessly for more than an hour, they returned to Teague's garage. Still, Baye was surprised at how stiff her back and legs were when she climbed off the bike again. She stumbled a little as she dismounted and might have fallen if Teague hadn't grabbed her arm to steady her.

"Whoa. I didn't expect to be so stiff."

"Did I go too far? I should have told you to tap me on the shoulder when you wanted to return." Teague spoke quickly, appearing anxious. Baye was beginning to realize Teague was self-assured about her intellect but apparently needed constant reassurance when interacting with people.

Baye laughed. "No. Our ride was perfect." She stretched her legs and did a few twisting stretches to loosen her back. "It's like riding a horse when you haven't for a while. You feel fine while you're mounted, not realizing until you dismount and try to walk that the muscles you've been working aren't in shape anymore."

"Then you enjoyed our ride?" Teague engaged the kickstand and dismounted. She placed her helmet on a short shelf and hung the leather jacket she was wearing on a hook below it.

"Yes! It was fantastic. I wish we'd been on an old airstrip so you could have gone even faster." She held out her helmet for Teague to stow.

Teague took the helmet and frowned. "Even though this model can go well over two hundred miles per hour, I would never go that fast while carrying a passenger."

Her response did nothing to calm Baye's exuberance or dissuade her from giving Teague a tight hug. "Of course you wouldn't." She drew her keys from her pocket. "Although I hate to end our visit, it's almost feeding time at the rescue."

"Here, too," Teague said as she walked Baye to her SUV and opened the unlocked door on the driver's side for her to climb in.

Normally, such chivalry would seem uncomfortably butch to Baye, but Teague was different. The gesture was simply true to her personality and didn't come off as masculine. She suddenly remembered something and lowered her window. "Hey, you said something earlier today about a proposal."

"Yes. A financial arrangement I would like to hammer out with you." Teague looked at the ground for a quick minute, then glanced up at Baye. "Now is not a good time since we both have animals waiting to be fed, and my offer requires a bit of explanation. However, if you are not busy Thursday night, perhaps you could return and have dinner with me."

She frowned. "You're going to make me wait three days before you tell me about this mysterious deal you want to offer me?"

Teague wrinkled her brow and shrugged. "Thursday is my birthday. I am sure Connie will make a fuss over it—baking a cake and cooking my favorite food."

"Oh." Baye pursed her lips. Teague had said she didn't have any friends. Would she spend her birthday alone if Baye didn't accept her invitation? "Hmm. I'd be glad to share your birthday dinner with you, as long as your favorite food isn't something weird like octopus or kidney pie."

Teague's smile broadened. "No. It is liver and onions."

Baye widened her eyes and shook her head. "At least the company will be good."

Teague laughed. "I am making a joke. My favorite food is a veggie burger and steak fries."

"Are you a vegetarian?"

"No. I just happen to like this specific brand of veggie burger better than meat. I can have Connie prepare a regular burger for you."

"No." She took a second to rethink her answer. "Well, it wouldn't hurt to have one at the ready, but I'd like to try one of your veggie burgers first."

"Then you will accept my invitation?"

"I'm looking forward to it." She really, really was.

❖

"You're late. I have to go to work, so John has started feeding the dogs." Libby glared at Baye. "This is the third time this week that either John or I has had to feed. The evening feeding is your job, Baye. John gets up at daybreak to clean pens, do the morning feed, and keep up all the landscape and maintenance work around here. And I have a second-shift job, so I can't do it."

"I'm sorry. I was making up with our neighbor. She says she has a financial proposal for me."

"What does that mean? What's she proposing?"

"I'll find out Thursday. She's invited me to her birthday dinner."

Libby snorted. "Like she's going to talk business at her birthday party."

"I don't think it's a party. She apparently doesn't have a lot of friends…well, not human friends. I think it will just be the two of us."

Libby raised an eyebrow. "Maybe she wants to pay you to be a friend-with-benefits."

She scowled. "She's not like that. She's sweet, and chivalrous, and very rule oriented. She's just awkward and unsure with people."

Libby slipped her laptop into her messenger bag. "I hope you're right, and she makes a big donation to Heavy Petting." She paused by the front door. "We really need to hire someone to help John, which you should be doing right now."

"I'm going, I'm going."

"You also need to update our website and social media. Someone dumped two new dogs on us while you were out having fun, and you need to delete the pets that found families at the adoption event Saturday."

"I will," she said, but they both knew Libby would have to prompt her several more times to get that work done. She was just so easily distracted. And her neighbor with the intense eyes and sexy body was a big distraction.

CHAPTER SEVEN

Teague swiped her finger through the bowl of cream-cheese frosting, narrowly dodging a crack on the knuckles from Connie's wooden spoon.

"If you don't quit, I'm not going to have enough to ice the cake." Connie's scolding drew a frown from Teague.

"I do not know why you bother with a cake," she said. "Just stick a couple of candles in the icing."

"I might do that if you weren't having an adult guest for dinner," Connie said. "I don't want her to think she's dining with a six-year-old."

Teague made a dismissive sound. She was not aware of a rule against licking bowls once you reached adult age. She stole another fingerful of icing, but Connie's spoon was quick this time. "Ow!"

"Behave." Connie placed the second layer of cake on top of the first, then poured the frosting from the bowl on top. She handed the empty bowl and a spoon to Teague, who instantly began devouring the leavings. She loved cream-cheese frosting. Connie shook her head as she spread the icing over the entire cake. "Are you sure about the menu? Maybe your friend would like something fancier."

"Nope. I did promise to have a meat burger in case she doesn't like my Beyond Burger." She went to the sink to rinse the frosting bowl and put it in the dishwasher. The rote move was partly due to her need for order and partly because nothing left out was safe with a monkey in the house.

"Good idea. I'll cook both." Connie was quiet as she washed and chopped potatoes for steak fries. "I'm a little surprised you wanted to acknowledge your fortieth birthday, considering you see it as a harbinger of your early demise."

Teague frowned. "Who told you that?"

"Margaret called the day after the funeral to ask if you were okay. She was worried after revealing your birth father."

She pinned Connie with an indignant stare. "You knew, and you did not tell me?" The betrayal burned her. She had forgiven her great-aunt's silence, but Connie was more like her second mother. How could she have kept this from her? She stood and paced angrily.

"Oh, honey. It was your parents' decision to keep your adoption secret. They didn't want the idea of that supposed curse hanging over you all your life and asked me to honor their decision." She wiped her hands on a dish cloth and rounded the kitchen island to intercept Teague's pacing and hug her tightly from behind. "You've been like a daughter to me since you were a baby, and I don't believe in that stupid curse. I think your father and his brother brought their deaths on themselves by smoking cigars and never exercising."

She stopped pacing and relaxed in Connie's prolonged hug. "I have called my doctor about getting an MRI."

Connie released her, then tugged her around to face her. "Do what you feel you must to ease your mind, but please don't dwell on this. You are healthy as a horse, and now you have this pretty friend right next door."

"I want to talk to her about finding homes for my animals when I am gone."

"Not Badger." The little terrier mix at Connie's feet wagged his tail. "Nothing is going to happen to you, but if I'm still alive when you do leave this life, that little guy is mine."

Teague smiled, her anxiety draining away. "I promise. You already own his heart. Have you been slipping him extra treats?" She was teasing Connie.

"I plead the Fifth." Connie retrieved a large bowl of fresh strawberries from the refrigerator and handed it to it to Teague. "Clean and wash these, please."

"I have to prepare my own birthday dinner?"

"You have to help if you want your cake topped with strawberries..." Connie paused chopping up the potatoes.

A carrot cake with cream-cheese frosting and strawberries. It was an odd combination, but Teague's favorite. She moved to the sink to begin the task.

"Truthfully, I need to keep you busy here in the house or you'll disappear into that animal house and get busy writing equations, and your guest will end up eating cake by herself."

"The cottage is my office, not an animal house. And I think better with them close by."

It was true. Leo's deep purr when he was sprawled across her desk for a belly rub warmed her, as did Flower's pleased grunts as Teague scratched behind her ears. Cappie and Mac arguing over food, then Cappie grooming Mac like he was another monkey and Mac careful with his huge beak as he reciprocated entertained her. And Snow's soft snores as he rested up for his night guard duty calmed her.

"I know, sweetie." Connie sprinkled the potatoes with seasoning, then dumped them into the air fryer. "Although I complain a lot about them, I do care about your beasts. I'd offer to live here with them if something did happen to you, but most of them would outlive me. What would happen to them then? You need a better solution."

"That is my plan."

❖

Baye was surprised when Connie answered the door instead of Teague. She was much more welcoming than the first time she'd found Baye on their doorstep. "Is…is Teague here?"

Connie grabbed her hand and practically dragged her through the doorway. "Yes. She's expecting you. Come on back to the kitchen."

Teague, however, wasn't there. A cake topped with strawberries and two candles shaped in a four and a zero sat on the table, and Badger was the only animal present.

"Your timing is perfect," Connie said, taking a tray of three burgers from the oven. "I had just put these in the oven to keep warm, and the steak fries need only another minute or two."

Baye shifted uncomfortably. "Is she out back in the cottage?"

"No, dear. She's in her rooms." Connie pointed to a door near the diaper-changing station. "I gave her a nice shirt for her birthday and insisted she wear it to your date rather than that ratty T-shirt she had on. I thought she'd pay more attention to her attire once she grew up, but it's still like pulling teeth to get her to wear a collared shirt unless she has a business meeting. Have a seat while I finish the food preparations."

Baye climbed onto one of the padded stools at the kitchen island and held up a gift bag she'd brought. "I hope she likes the present I got for her. It was a hard choice. We've been friends only a little more than a week, and I imagine she buys herself anything she really wants, so it was hard to decide." She hesitated. "Did she say this was a date?"

"No. She'd never admit that. I could tell, though, that she's a little anxious about making a good impression."

"Me, too." Baye was relieved she wasn't the only one feeling nervous. She fidgeted a bit. "I really like her. We're totally opposite in many ways, but alike in others. We both struggle for people to understand and accept us." She ignored Connie's raised eyebrow encouraging her to explain more.

After a long moment, Connie lowered her voice. "Well, I can give you a few pointers where she's concerned."

"Please. That would help."

"She generally doesn't like other people touching her, but if you wrap your arms around her in a firm hug a minute longer than most would think appropriate, you'll feel her relax and hug back."

"I think I figured that one out already, riding behind her on the motorcycle the other day."

"Also, you must be explicit with her. She has trouble recognizing subtleties in other people's expressions and body language. You might have to say you do or don't like something. And, when she's tired or hungry, she gets more impatient and less understanding—"

At the sound of a door opening behind Baye, Connie abruptly turned and opened the drawer of the air fryer. "Oh, dear. I've been chatting away like an old fool and almost cooked the steak fries too long."

Baye felt a fleeting touch to her back. "Hey, you," she said as she turned to face Teague, and her breath caught. "Wow. You clean up nice." Suddenly unsure how Teague might interpret the cliché, she remembered Connie's advice to be specific and added, "You are devastatingly handsome in that shirt."

Teague's face reddened. "It is a birthday present from Connie. I am wearing it to please her."

Baye eyed the dark blue Oxford shirt left untucked over faded jeans. "That disappoints me. I was hoping you were wearing it to please me." She stepped forward and wrapped Teague in a tight hug for a long moment, then kissed her on the cheek before stepping back. "Happy Birthday."

Teague glanced at her and reached up to touch the cheek Baye had kissed. "I, uh—"

When she couldn't seem to find the words, Connie interrupted her. "You two have a nice dinner." She loaded her meal and a carafe of hot herbal tea onto a serving cart. "I'm going to have mine in my rooms upstairs so I can put my feet up and watch my television shows."

"Would you like us to bring you a slice of cake when we cut it?" Baye asked.

"Thank you, dear, but the sugar would keep me awake. I'll have a slice in the morning for breakfast." She pushed the cart past the ornate wrought-iron door that kept the animals—except for Badger, who happily followed at her heels—from entering the rest of the house, then touched a black button on her left, and the wall opened up. Connie, her dinner cart, and the little terrier stepped into the elevator that was revealed and were gone.

"Connie lives upstairs? Is Badger her dog or yours?"

Teague smiled and held up her finger. "I can answer only one question at a time, but we should eat before our food is cold." She took their plates from the oven and carried them over to a bistro table set for two. "Would you like a glass of wine or a beer?"

"I'll have whatever you're drinking."

"I do not drink alcohol. I am having water with my meal."

"That sounds perfect." Baye was curious but would ask later why Teague didn't drink. She held out a chair for her to be seated.

Teague frowned. "I should seat you as a guest in my house."

"But you are the birthday girl, so I thought I should seat you."

Teague seemed to ponder this response, then sat in the offered chair, only to spring back up. "No. This does not feel right." She held out the opposite chair for Baye. "Please let me seat you."

Baye started to protest, then sat down. "It's your birthday, so you get anything you want." She allowed Teague to settle her closer to the table. "How has your day been so far?"

"Productive. I cleared my inbox, accepted a new contract that I will sign after my attorney checks it, and had the shearer out this afternoon to give Lucky and the Fluffy family their summer haircuts."

"The Fluffy family?"

"My three sheep."

Baye covered her mouth as she laughed. She managed to chew and swallow without spraying her bite of veggie burger across the table. "Cotton, Crochet, and Yarn. I love it. Do you personally name all your animals?" More than half had names unexpectedly humorous, considering their very serious owner.

"Mac, Cappie, and Leo came with their names. Asset belonged to a goat herder who was selling his farm. He called him Stupid, but I thought that carried a negative connotation and renamed him Asset." She held up her hand. "I do not believe animals understand the meanings of their names, but they are very sensitive to tone."

Baye cocked her head and wrinkled her brow, trying to understand what Teague was explaining. "Tone?"

"Yes. The farmer would call out 'Hey, Stupid.' Asset is a positive word, and people naturally use a friendlier tone when they say it. I believe the animal reacts to the happier tone, and the person also unconsciously responds to the positive vibe."

Baye swallowed the last of her burger and pointed to her plate. "This veggie burger, by the way, was delicious."

"I am happy you like it." Teague swished a steak fry back and forth through the ketchup she poured onto her plate. "Flower had simply been called Pig."

"That's not a good name for a lady swine. I imagine Flower makes her feel pretty."

Teague nodded. "You think of something pretty when you say it, and she obviously reacts to that cue. Pigs are very intelligent."

"I imagine the sheep didn't have names, just a number if they came from a rancher."

Teague nodded while she chewed.

"I never thought about this subject before, but I agree. Now I'm thinking over the names of the animals we've taken in at Heavy Petting. I might need to change some of them." She chewed a steak fry as she considered this possibility. "All of the rescue places have an overload of pit bulls, and a lot of them have intimidating names. I'll bet we'd be able to adopt more of them if we gave them friendlier names. I think I'll change Terminator's name to Teddy."

Teague nodded again, finishing her burger. "You would not want to adopt out a dog to a person who liked Terminator as a name anyway. Those people tend to seek breeds that they can train to be aggressive. Most pits are sweet, loyal dogs that are good with children and cats if they are raised correctly."

Baye was mesmerized by this socially isolated genius. She'd already discovered a very big heart and hidden surprises, like a daredevil motorcyclist, under that stiff, formal exterior. And, obviously, the way to Teague's heart was through her animal friends. The sexual chemistry practically crackled between them, but Teague had made no real move to encourage it. Instinct told Baye that she'd have to make the first move, but she was hesitant. If she was too forward, Teague might run faster than Miss Hennie when mealworms and sunflower seeds were thrown out into the barnyard.

Teague glanced up just as each of them put a steak fry in her mouth, and they smiled at each other as they chewed. Yep. Definite chemistry.

❖

"Are you ready for cake?" Uneasy with the reminder of her age, Teague reached to remove and set aside the candles shaped like a four and a zero from the top of the cake.

"Don't take those off," Baye said, grabbing Teague's arm to stop her. "We have to light them and sing happy birthday to you." She looked around. "And where is everybody?"

Teague was puzzled. "Connie is upstairs. She said she will have cake in the morning."

"No. Not Connie. Where are Cappie, Flower, Mac, and the rest? They're family, too. We have to share your birthday with them as well."

How can she explain this? "Mac and Cappie are in their sunroom cages, and the rest are outdoors in the barn or pasture. Connie said their tendency to beg and sometimes try to steal food from the table would not be appropriate when I have a dinner guest."

"I'm not just any dinner guest." She reached across the table, causing Teague to flinch when she grabbed her hand and held on to it. "I love your animals, and they are family to you. So, let them share this with us." Baye let go of her hand and indicated the door to the sunroom, which led out onto a large terrace. "Should we move outside so everybody can join us?"

Teague blinked in surprise, but delight bloomed in her chest. The last woman she'd invited to dinner had fled halfway through the meal because of the animals. "Are you sure?"

"Absolutely." Baye stood, picked up the cake, and headed for the door. "You bring out plates and a cloth to wipe off the patio table," she called over her shoulder.

Teague hurriedly gathered the dessert plates, a knife for cutting the cake, and a damp dishcloth to clean the table. The minute she stepped into the sunroom, Cappie jumped from the top of his cage to her shoulder, and she nearly tripped over Mac, who was toddling across the floor in pursuit of Baye, who had obviously opened both cages on her way to the terrace.

Outside, she found the cake abandoned on the table and Baye unlatching the pasture gate for the pasture residents that might want to join them. Flower and Leo trotted toward them from the cottage. The Fluffy family and Lucky the llama lay in the grass and watched with interest, but apparently they preferred their own cud-chewing party.

It was a raucous gathering—Flower squealing, the goats bleating, Asset braying, Snow barking, and Mac yelling "cake" to summon his buddies until Baye made a slashing motion and yelled, "Quiet."

To Teague's amazement, the animals fell silent. "They never listen to me like that," she said, frowning.

"Okay, everybody," Baye said to the menagerie. "We're going to light the candles and sing 'Happy Birthday' to Teague."

"Happy Birthday," Mac said. "Happy Birthday."

"Yes, thank you, Mac," Baye said as she lit the two candles. "Now, let's sing."

Teague's arms broke out in goose bumps as Baye's rich, melodic alto rang out. Then she laughed when the animals joined in. Mac knew the song but liked to draw out the "to you" in a long warble, Flower squealed her part, Abigail, Tater, and Tot bleated, and Snow howled when Asset's bray joined the cacophony. To discourage a second round of their "singing," she blew out the candles before the first round ended.

Baye handed her the knife. "Cut a big serving for Connie, and I'll take it to the kitchen while you slice pieces for you and me."

"Put it in the refrigerator so Mac and Cappie do not sneak into the house and eat it." Teague waved a threatening finger at her resident thieves.

The animals got slices proportionate to their sizes on small paper plates, and when Baye returned, she and Teague stood to eat theirs since Cappie and Mac were occupying the only two chairs.

"Oh my God." Baye's loud exclamation startled Teague so much, she almost dropped her plate.

"What?" Her heart beating wildly, Teague scanned the yard for signs of trouble.

"This cake is so-o-o good. I like carrot cake, but I love cream-cheese frosting."

Teague put her hand to her chest, to calm the thumping inside, and looked down in time to see Cappie had finished his serving and was plucking the strawberries from the top of the cake and sharing them with Mac. "Cappie. Stop that." The monkey chattered at her, unfazed by her stern scolding while he snacked on the last juicy treat. She was aghast at his bad manners, but Baye only laughed.

"Relax. They're celebrating, too," she said, handing the last strawberry on the cake to Mac. She cut another slice of cake for Flower, who squealed and wagged her tail like a dog when Baye placed it before her.

Teague was a little surprised, but a lot pleased, that Baye was so thoughtful with the animals. The few women who tried to date Teague had turned out to love her money much more than the animals. They all wanted to go out to fancy restaurants.

Baye put her hand to her mouth, her eyes wide. "Should I have asked before I gave Flower a second helping? It won't hurt her, will it?"

She frowned at Flower's smacking as she enjoyed her cake. "I usually watch her diet. Most people are not aware a two-hundred-pound, pot-bellied pig can quickly become a six-hundred-pound pig if they are fed everything they want." She smiled at Baye's anxious expression. "But everybody gets a free day from their diet occasionally, right?"

Baye's uncertain expression transformed into a broad grin. "Absolutely. Can Asset, Abigail, and the kids have more?"

Teague considered this possibility. "Carrot cake already has a lot of sugar in it, and the frosting adds even more." She raised an eyebrow at Baye. This woman inexplicably made Teague feel playful, an emotion foreign except on rare occasions when she was interacting with the animals. "Perhaps we should eat the frosting and give them the cake part. It does have carrots in it."

Baye's expression was one of pure delight. "Why, Ms. Maxwell! I believe there's a child hiding behind that serious genius." She scraped her fork across the top of the remaining cake and rolled her eyes in dramatic appreciation when she licked the cream-cheese icing from it. "So-o-o good."

"So-o-o good," Mac echoed, strawberry bits hanging from his mouth.

"Forget the cake and strawberries. I'd be happy with a bowl of this frosting and a spoon." She devoured another forkful from the cake and savored it. "This is not a criticism of Connie's fantastic cake, but—" She froze, her fork poised for another dive into the frosting, and stared at Teague. "Oh my God. You must be horrified at my poor manners."

"Not at all." Teague happily scraped her fork down the side of the cake. She was not the only adult who turned into a kid when it came to cake icing. "I was waiting for my turn because I was afraid I could be stabbed by your fast-moving fork."

Baye's mouth dropped open. "You made a joke!"

Teague froze with her fork still in her mouth, then slowly pulled it out and swallowed. Had she said something inappropriate?

Baye let loose a delighted laugh. "I wish I had a mirror so you could see your face."

Teague relaxed a bit, but heat crawled up her neck to her ears. "I did not intend to offend you."

"No. No. It was funny. You just caught me by surprise because I can't remember you making a joke before."

"Oh." She mentally reviewed everything they'd said in the past few minutes, committing it to memory so maybe she could figure out how to make a joke again. Getting Baye to laugh was becoming her new life mission—what was left of her life.

They scraped the remaining frosting from the cake, then served it to the animals. Asset chomped noisily until his treat was gone, then snuffled the grass below, searching for dropped crumbs. Abigail, Tater, and Tot ate theirs more slowly, making contented little bleating sounds as they chewed.

"I have a financial proposal for you…well, for the rescue center."

"Finally. I've been dying of curiosity. Let's hear it."

"Would you walk with me? I need to put the animals in the barn, then check that the chickens have returned to their coop there." She took out her phone and hit the speed dial for Connie. "Please send Badger down. It will start raining soon, and I want to bring everybody in from the pasture. Thank you."

When she returned Mac and Cappie to their sunroom cages, Flower settled onto a nearby fluffy dog bed as Badger appeared. "Bring them in, Badger," she said, and the dog sprinted for the pasture gate with Snow loping behind him.

Dusk had fallen and the air was heavy with the promise of rain. The path to the pasture gate had a slight incline, and when Baye slipped in the damp grass, Teague grabbed her arm without thinking.

"Thanks. I should have worn more sensible shoes," Baye said, looking down at her ballet-style flats with a leather sole.

Teague grimaced. "Those do not look comfortable or durable."

Baye shook her head. "They are pretty comfortable, but not made to tramp through wet grass."

Teague stopped. "You should have said you were not wearing proper shoes for a walk. You could wait on the terrace while I tend to the animals."

"No. I want to help you tuck everybody in for the night."

Touching Baye felt natural, unlike when anyone else touched her. She only tolerated the hugs from Aunt Margaret and Connie, even though they knew how to touch her. Small touches made her flinch away, so she surprised herself by hooking Baye's arm in hers to keep her steady and slowing their pace. Baye smelled faintly of lavender, which was good because Teague couldn't tolerate strong scents, and her silk blouse felt cool against Teague's skin.

Badger squeezed through the bars in the aluminum gate, but Snow waited for her to unlatch and open it. He was big enough to jump it, but she had taught him to wait because she feared he might slip and get his leg caught. She held the gate open for Baye, Asset, and the goats, and they all went into the barn.

"So…your proposal?"

Before Teague could answer her, Badger and Snow guided the sheep into the barn, with Lucky the llama trailing behind.

"Let's get everyone settled first." She went into the feed room and returned with two small scoops of feed and handed them to Baye. "Can you put one in the goats' feed pan and the other in the sheep stall? You can refill one of your scoops from the trash can marked as rabbit feed and give that to them."

Everybody hurried into their assigned pens without prompting. Lucky and Asset went into their stalls and waited while Teague dropped a scoop of feed into their buckets and slid their doors closed. The chickens filed into their coop, which was enclosed with hardware cloth to keep out any predators, like snakes or rats, that might slip past Snow. Teague checked for eggs, then filled their feeder. The hens pecked at the food a bit, then began to settle in their individual nests for the night.

All the stalls had automatic water devices, but she checked to make sure none were malfunctioning and everybody had clean water. When she finished, she realized Baye hadn't come out of the rabbits' pen. She found her sitting with a rabbit on either side of her while she stroked their backs and scratched around their ears.

She looked up at Teague. "Their fur is so incredibly soft."

"They love to be petted. Both are old men, destined for the butcher when I rescued them."

"How do you find these animals?"

"There is an auction yard about two hours from here. Cattle, horses, and pigs are primarily for sale, but they occasionally have other animals like goats, sheep, rabbits, and chickens. I do not go very often because I find it stressful. Many are in bad condition because they have not been cared for properly."

Baye's eyes filled with tears. "I don't think I could go there. It would break my heart, and I'd want to bring every one of them home with me."

Teague hadn't meant to make her sad. She wanted her to laugh again. "Wait here a minute." She went to the feed room and returned with several rabbit toys. "Since they must stay inside tonight because of the weather, I will give them some toys for entertainment." She tossed out several balls woven from thin willow sticks, two small wreaths made of dry clover, and a couple of small bowls. The rabbits immediately ran to claim a toy.

"Are those wooden bowls? Do you put something in them?"

"They are made from palm leaves. All the toys are edible and will entertain them for hours." She sat on the floor next to Baye—close enough to breathe in her scent and feel the heat of her body, but not touching. "Rabbits need to chew on things that will wear down their front teeth or they must be filed down, which is not pleasant. In the wild, they chew wood and tough stems to keep them from growing too long."

They watched as one rabbit began collecting the toys in one corner, but when he went to retrieve another, the other rabbit raided his stash and took one to his own pile of toys.

Baye laughed. "They don't know how to share, do they?"

"It is a game they will play before settling down to chew one. Then the stealing begins again until they stop and chew another one. Sometimes they have a tugging contest over the willow balls. They will share if only one toy is left."

They both flinched when a loud boom of thunder sounded overhead, then relaxed with the comforting drum of rain against the barn's metal roof.

How to approach this situation? Teague mentally played out multiple scenarios for opening the subject of her proposal. How much should she reveal? She cleared her throat. "I need to find homes for my animals."

Baye turned to her and stared. "Can you repeat that? I'm pretty sure I heard you wrong."

Teague kept her eyes on the rabbits. She hadn't anticipated that taking the first step to implement her plan would make her chest hurt. Having finished his bowl of kibble in the feed room, Leo jumped back into the rabbits' pen and rubbed his big head against her shoulder. She pulled him into her lap and began to stroke his fur to calm herself. "I need to find new homes for my animals."

Baye put her hand to her mouth, then whispered, "Are you sick?"

She shook her head. "Not at the moment, but no one on my father's side of the family lived to see their forty-first birthday. All died of aneurysms. Our family believes we are cursed. I am having tests soon to search for any weakened vessels around my heart and brain as a precaution. Regardless of the outcome, I need to be prepared."

She could feel Baye's gaze boring into her, but she didn't comment, so Teague continued. "I want to put you…your rescue center on retainer to find new homes for them—homes that I approve."

Baye's eyebrows shot up. "Retainer?"

"Three thousand a month, paid in advance each month for you to rehome my animals." She held her hand up to silence Baye when she started to speak. "I am aware that most have come to live with me for reasons that made them hard to place, and those reasons will make them hard to rehome now. That's why I am asking to put you on retainer so you can hire someone to feed and clean up at your rescue while you concentrate on finding appropriate homes for my crew."

Baye waved her hands in front of her. "Wait, wait. Three thousand dollars?"

"Okay. How about five? You could hire two people, or hire one and use the rest for food or vet services."

Baye couldn't believe what she was hearing. "Stop. Just stop, and let me digest this." She stood and paced, careful not to step on the rabbits, who had settled down to gnaw on their toys. "You're not sick, but you're sure you'll die within the next year? I would have never pegged you for superstitious."

"I am not superstitious. My eminent death is based on a statical calculation derived from empirical evidence." Teague also stood, her arms crossed over her chest.

"What if your MRI shows you're perfectly healthy?"

"Aneurysms are not always detectable in advance. My father

had an MRI and a cardiac stress test, but he still died of a brain aneurysm two months later."

"Maybe he should have gone to a more reliable hospital."

"He went to the Mayo Clinic."

Baye's frustration bloomed. Despite her outwardly gregarious personality, she had very few real friends once they experienced the impact of her disability, and she had felt like Teague could become a close friend because she understood being limited by a disability that people found hard to understand. "I don't believe you're going to die. You're standing here, as healthy as a person can be. Thinking that you're going to die at any minute must be stressful. You need your animals. I've known you only a short time, but I can see how they ground you. This is the worst possible time for you to give them away."

"Are you turning down my proposal?"

"No. I'm not. I just need to think about it for a minute." Baye paced again. This notion of impending death was ridiculous, but the center desperately needed the money. Working with Teague on this undertaking also would give them more time together, which was a shit reason for accepting her offer. On the other hand, Teague would just hire someone else if she refused. "Okay. I'll do it."

Teague nodded, appearing solemn. "Thank you. Unless you have someone in mind, I can ask Bruce if he knows a vet student like him you could hire for kennel help."

"Yes, please. That would be helpful." Her head was swimming with the thought of an extra five thousand dollars a month, but she wasn't good at figuring finances. That's what Libby did. "What do you pay Bruce?"

"I pay him five hundred a week for about twenty hours of work. He feeds and cleans the barn and sunroom twice a day, keeps inventory of the feed room, and orders more when needed. He works Monday through Friday and two Saturdays a month unless we need to change something to work around his school schedule."

Baye nodded. That was only two thousand. Her mind whirled with idea of three thousand still left to spend. "That sounds fair."

"We'll have to make a run for it through the rain, but let's go to my office so I can transfer the money to Heavy Petting."

"I don't have my account information. I'd have to get it from home. That seems like a lot of money to find homes for a handful of pets."

"It will be more difficult and time-consuming than you might think," Teague said, opening the door to step out of the rabbit pen, then closing it behind them. "You'll see when we sit down to discuss each animal and the things that make them hard to adopt. And if you have an Apple or Venmo account, I can send it there so I won't need your bank account information."

Baye was both excited about the money and sad at the thought of separating Teague from any of her animals. "I'll find them the best homes—" Lightning lit up the night visible through the open doors of the barn, immediately followed by a loud crack and a boom of thunder that shook the building. A blood-curdling shriek, Snow's sharp barks, and Asset's terrified brays filled the barn as residual electricity from the lightning strike raised the hair on her arms. The noise…it was too much.

"Shit, shit, shit. Motherfucker." Baye screamed the curses. "We could be killed." Adrenaline burst through her system, and she ran for the nearest open door, only to realize she was headed straight for a still-smoking tree. She wheeled to run back, chanting loudly. "Lightning doesn't strike twice. Lightning doesn't strike twice." Then her panic went from a hundred to zero when she spotted Teague sitting against the wall of Asset's stall, curled into a tight ball. She held her hands tight over her ears and had her eyes closed. Baye dropped to her knees next to her. "Teague, are you hurt? Did the lightning get you?" She'd heard it could travel through the ground. Was that true?

"Too loud. Too much," Teague said through gritted teeth.

Snow had moved close to Teague as if protecting her, and Baye ran her hands over his thick coat to calm him. "Shush,

Snow. It's okay." Then she stood and reached into Asset's stall to quiet him. The chickens settled, too, as the noise subsided.

When all was quiet except for the rain pounding the roof, she knelt again and spoke in a low, soothing tone. "Teague, honey. Can I touch you, or do you just need time?"

Teague's arms were wrapped around her bent legs and her forehead held tightly against her knees. She mumbled something Baye couldn't understand, so she moved her ear as close to Teague's head as possible without touching her. "Can you say that again, please."

"Hug."

Baye nodded but moved slowly to wrap her arms around Teague in a firm embrace. She could feel Teague's heart beating wildly and held on as she felt it slow.

"I am okay now." Teague's voice was shaky.

Baye slowly released her, and they stood. They both stared at the huge oak now split in two near the barn's open doors. "I'm glad all the animals are safe in the barn," she said.

"Yes." Teague turned away, wiping her forehead with a trembling hand. "We must go to the cottage." She headed into the downpour in a fast walk, leaving Baye to follow.

"Okay," Baye said, drawing the word out under her breath. She hesitated at the entrance to the barn, then plunged into the rain.

Chapter Eight

Teague didn't run, but she fled her mortification with every long stride. It had literally been years since she had a meltdown in front of someone else. Unmindful of the rain, she mentally played out at least twenty scenarios that would allow her to back out of the proposed deal she'd just presented to Baye. She'd always been overly sensitive to loud sounds and overpowering smells, but Mac's occasional screeching calls, Flower's intermittent squeals, and Asset's loud braying had mostly desensitized her. Damn it. She was forty years old, yet she had curled up like a small child when the lightning strike sparked the frightened cacophony from her animals.

She went directly to her desk and retrieved the laptop hidden in the center drawer from her more curious pets. She was typing in the web address for the rescue center and didn't look up when Baye walked through the door. "Are you sure you want to do this? Most of my pets will be hard to place, especially with the contracts I am going to require to ensure they live out their lives with the same care and freedom I have provided."

Baye didn't answer but walked to the whiteboard covered with a complicated mathematical equation. "I can't even fathom the depth of your genius. This looks like a foreign language."

"It would appear so to anyone who is not a physicist." Thunder rolled overhead again, but almost thirty seconds after the flash of lightning. The storm was moving away, yet the rain hadn't let up. Teague banged her fist on the desk. "Damn internet is out."

"That's okay," Baye said. "You might change your mind about hiring me after I tell you something about myself."

Teague didn't respond but turned enough to see Baye without looking directly at her, which didn't matter because Baye, still staring at the whiteboard, had her back to her.

"I have severe attention-deficit/hyperactivity disorder. I've been fired from most jobs I've held because I was chronically late or left a task unfinished because something else distracted me, or I had a meltdown where I went off on a coworker or my supervisor. I like you a lot and hope we can be friends, so I need you to know about my disability and understand my daily struggle."

Teague's thoughts raced to the misunderstanding they'd had the week after the adopt-a-thon. Baye's reaction had been a bit over the top. Baye still hadn't turned to face her, so Teague typed in a quick search for ADHD when the internet connection rebooted and blinked in surprise at the endless number of websites offering information. She read quickly while Baye continued.

"ADHD isn't a disability like missing a limb or having a muscular disease, so a lot of people see me as lazy, reckless, impulsive, self-centered, and overly emotional. After a while, they find a friendship with me is too much work and either drift away or get mad and cut me out of their lives."

Baye's voice had grown closer, and Teague finally glanced up to worried hazel eyes. She cleared her throat. "I am very high functioning but diagnosed as autistic. Like you, my brain works differently than most people's. It is a disadvantage because people do not understand me and make fun of my speech, but it is also a gift because I often can see problems and their solutions from a different perspective."

"That's why you don't like crowds, or people in general. And you don't like to be touched."

She nodded but couldn't hold Baye's gaze and looked down

when she felt Snow press against her legs. "Where you might be constantly distracted when trying to complete a project or task, I tend to be super focused. When I am working to solve a problem, I often forget to eat or sleep for days. Connie watches out for that tendency and will not let me go more than a day without rest and nourishment."

"My grandmother left the farm to me and Libby because she knew the rescue center wouldn't be a success without Libby to rein in my spending impulses. She manages our finances."

Heat crawled up Teague's neck and flooded her cheeks. "I am sensitive to certain scents like heavy perfumes and cannot tolerate loud sounds like earlier." Baye's hand on her shoulder ratcheted up her internal heat wave, scorching her ears as well. "The lightning strike and the noise from the frightened animals surpassed the limit I can tolerate."

"Oh, honey. I'm so sorry. It startled me, and my scream might have set the animals off, not to mention my very vocal meltdown."

Teague nodded. "You have a potty mouth."

Baye laughed. "Yes, I do when I'm stressed. I'm trying to get better at that." She averted her eyes, and her cheeks flushed pink. "Sometimes I get overwhelmed and lose control of my emotions. I've lost jobs, friends, and family support because of it."

Teague relaxed a bit. Could they be more different, yet so similar? "My animals are my friends, and my great-aunt is the only family member who understands me. Connie is not a relative, but I consider her to be family. They both know when and how to touch me." The lightning incident still puzzled her. "They know not to touch me when I…when I become overwhelmed."

Baye withdrew as if she was just now aware of her hand on Teague's shoulder. "Sorry. I forgot about the touching thing."

"No." Teague grabbed her hand. "For some reason, your touch does not bother me." She entwined her fingers with Baye's. "When you hugged me in the barn, it calmed me instead of escalating my distress."

Baye's smile was slow and her expression shy as she ducked her head. "You seem to be my lightning rod, too. Touching you drains away my anxiety and grounds me."

Teague stood and tugged Baye to the door. "The rain has let up. We should check on Mac in the sunroom."

"Do you have an umbrella?"

Teague tilted her head in thought, or maybe it was to let the water drain from her ears. "I do not think we need one since we are already soaked down to our underwear."

Baye's full-throated laugh both warmed Teague inside and cooled the flush from her skin. "See? You ground me. I would have spent thirty minutes looking for an umbrella before realizing I couldn't get any wetter than I already am."

❖

"Thank God you're both okay," Connie said. "I was coming to check on you after I heard that explosion. Then Badger ran in, frantic for me to follow him outside."

Mac's deafening screeches should have triggered another meltdown, but Teague only grinned when Baye began to laugh again. Connie looked as though she'd stepped out of a British comedy. She carried an enormous umbrella and wore a shower cap over her hair, a full-length yellow raincoat, and pink rubber boots.

"Lightning struck that big oak tree behind the barn, and it did startle us, but you running into the barn in that outfit might have scared us worse." Teague shouted to be heard over Mac's clamor, then held her arm out for him to step on, hugged him to her chest, and stroked his back to quiet him.

Cappie leapt onto Baye's shoulder. He wrapped his tail around her neck and burrowed into her long hair. "Poor Cappie. Did the storm frighten you? Or does Connie's storm-wear scare you?"

Connie squinted at them. "A couple of comedians, huh?"

Mac tilted his head as if just noticing Baye. "Hello, Pretty." He left Teague and climbed onto Baye's outstretched arm.

Connie made a dismissive but good-natured sound. "He never tells me I'm pretty."

"That is his name for Baye," Teague said. She looked at Baye, her light brown hair frizzed by the rain and her hazel eyes framed by long, dark lashes. "She *is* pretty."

"Yes. She is." Connie smiled and winked at Baye. "You girls are soaked. You should get into some dry clothes."

"Some dry clothes would be nice. Then I should go check on the animals at my place. John is there, but he's nearly deaf. As loud as that lightning strike was, he might not have even heard it if he has his hearing aids out."

"Teague, you have some freshly laundered sweats and T-shirts in your chest of drawers. They may be a little long on Baye but should do fine," Connie said. "Since I'm not going out, I should put my rain gear away. I'll say good night to you girls." She waved over her shoulder as she headed for her elevator with Badger trailing her.

Teague was suddenly uncertain. It had been an emotional night with their double meltdown, then their swapped confessions about their disabilities. Of course, talking about their handicaps wasn't the same as fully experiencing them. She was already bracing herself for their new relationship to blow up, but she couldn't bring herself to walk away like she'd done with other women. Although she'd dated a few women as an experiment, she was always relieved when they gave up their pursuit of her because of her aversion to touching and their dislike of her animal friends. "I have dry clothes—" She pointed at the door to her rooms.

"Lead the way," Baye said.

❖

Baye realized as she walked through a small sitting room that Teague, who owned this huge mansion, was living in the housekeeper's suite. The sitting room was apparently set up to handle late-night inspiration, with one wall covered by a huge whiteboard like the one in the cottage. The only furniture was a sofa, where Leo was grooming himself after the dash through the rain, and a standing desk, which held another laptop and faced the whiteboard. The bedroom held a king-sized bed, a night table, and a bookcase, and it had four doors—one to the sitting room, a second partially open to reveal a bathroom, and a third she expected led to the foyer so a housekeeper could quickly respond to a front-door visitor. Teague opened the fourth door and disappeared into a roomy walk-in closet.

While she was selecting some dry clothes for them both, Baye realized what seemed odd about the suite—the walls were bare, except for the whiteboard. No family photos. No artwork.

"These should fit you." Teague reappeared and held out a pair of nylon athletic pants and a T-shirt. She had a similar set for herself, along with dry underwear. "Uh, should I also offer you underwear?"

Baye shook her head, reading Teague's hesitation as reluctance to share such personal clothing. "No problem. I'll just go commando." She laid the pants and T-shirt on the bed and began to strip. Naked, she glanced up to reach for the pants and almost laughed at Teague, frozen and staring. She pretended not to notice but slowed her movements to let her look. She heard a door close as she pulled the T-shirt over her head and chuckled as the shirt cleared her head. Teague and her stack of dry clothes were gone, and the open bathroom door was now closed.

❖

Holy crap. Her escape to the bathroom felt foolish, but Teague's head was spinning, and her body was thrumming. She was forty years old, for God's sake, and an accomplished genius.

She had dated a couple of women in the past—the first was out of curiosity, and the second one had pursued her so vigorously that she had acquiesced to find out if her first foray into dating was uninspired because she'd chosen the wrong woman. She'd had sex with both, but only touched them intimately. She never let them touch her. And she'd never, *never* experienced the feelings and urges ignited by Baye's presence.

The image of naked Baye was burned on her brain. Her breasts were moderately full, where Teague's were small. A few inches shorter, Baye was curvy and smooth. Teague was six feet tall and slender to the point of sinewy, with wide shoulders and narrow hips. She itched to hold Baye's firm breasts, to thumb those pert nipples, and to run her hands over her soft skin and along her curves.

She changed quickly, checked her appearance in the mirror, then ran a brush through her dark hair. She inwardly cursed at her reflection. She saw straight, dark hair and plain brown eyes. She liked her boyish figure and had never worried over her appearance before, but she wished now that she had striking blue eyes or a more stylish haircut—something that made her more attractive. She cut her own hair to avoid having a strange hairdresser's hands on her.

She sucked in air, then blew out a deep breath. Time to face her new obsession.

❖

Baye sat on her bed when Teague exited the bathroom. "Can I ask you about something?"

Hesitantly, Teague nodded. "I will answer if I can." She hoped it would be a question about her proposal but braced herself for something more personal.

"Why do you stay in the housekeeper's quarters, and Connie stays upstairs in some of the family's rooms?"

She relaxed. This question was easy to answer. "I made a

deal with Connie for her rooms in exchange for prohibiting my menagerie from going into the rest of the house. Badger is the only exception because he and Connie seem to have bonded, and I promised to bathe him for her regularly or whenever he goes outside and gets muddy. As you can guess from the outside of the residence, this home is very large, professionally decorated, and contains heirlooms passed down through the family over many generations. I wanted my pets to have access to my rooms, so I persuaded Connie to move into my suite upstairs. Leo regularly sleeps on the bed with me, and Flower likes to be tucked into the dog bed in the corner."

Baye rose and opened the door to the foyer. "That was more detail than I expected, but thank you for explaining so thoroughly."

Her response pleased Teague, because most people grew impatient with her need for details. "Oh, and Connie finds the arrangement to her liking because she cannot hear Mac's late-night squawks from her rooms upstairs."

"I'll bet she's an early riser, so she goes to bed with the chickens, and you're the opposite."

"I do not sleep a lot and do not have to worry about waking her if I am up watching television shows I have recorded or rummaging in the kitchen for a late snack."

"Do you work in the sitting room much?"

"Occasionally, if I have a small inspiration. Any breakthrough or idea that advances my project significantly, I go out to the cottage." Teague realized that while they were talking, Baye had led her out the front door.

"I've enjoyed our time tonight so much I hate to leave, but I really must check on how everyone at my place weathered the storm."

"Do you want me to go with you?" Teague wasn't ready for their evening to end either, even though it was getting late.

"No. I'll be fine. I can roust out John if I need help with anything."

"Or you can call me. As you know, I can be there quickly since my house is next to yours." Teague didn't understand her need to be close to Baye and wasn't sure what to do about it.

"I know, but I'm exhausted after all the excitement. Everyone in the cathouse should be fine. I'll just need to check on the dogs and hand out calming pills to any that seem freaked out." When they reached Baye's car, she turned to Teague. "I'll see if Libby can meet with us tomorrow about your offer so we can work out the details, and then I'll text you to set a time."

"Okay." Teague studied her feet. "Thank you for sharing my birthday. I do not normally invite a guest." The hand on her face was cool, and Teague shifted her gaze to glance at Baye.

"It was my pleasure and an honor to be here," Baye said, her voice soft as she stepped close. "You are so sweet." Then Baye's lips were on hers, just a light brush until Teague pulled her closer for a firmer, lingering kiss.

She held Baye's gaze for a fleeting second when she finally stepped back and opened her SUV door. "I'll text you tomorrow," Baye said, her face flushed and eyes shining. And then she was gone.

Teague was transfixed as she watched the Subaru move slowly down her drive and turn left onto the roadway. The feelings Baye stirred in her were a cipher she wasn't sure how to solve. She was out of her element, stumbling with the onslaught of desire and unsure of her next step. It was late, but trying to sleep would be useless, so she headed for the cottage. She needed the familiarity of numbers and equations to ground her again.

❖

"What are you doing? Better question is what are you doing tomorrow?"

"I was doing what all other normal people do—sleeping." Libby's voice was hoarse, and her response was groggy. "And do you mean today? It's after midnight."

Baye switched the call to speaker and continued collecting trash from around the house. "I need to know when you can come by and meet with me and Teague tomorrow. We're going to get the money we need to keep the center open."

Libby seemed to perk up at that news. "Why? Is she giving us a big cash donation?"

"I kissed her."

Her declaration was answered with silence.

"She kissed me back."

"Okay. I'm willing to whore you out if it pays the bills." Libby's sarcasm was clear.

Baye flipped open a three-week-old pizza box that was on the coffee table. "Gross. I'm going to gag." Maggots were crawling among the moldy sausage and mushrooms.

Libby yawned. "What are you doing?"

"I'm cleaning up the house. Well, the downstairs anyway."

Another long silence. "Wow. She must be offering big money. I didn't know your girly parts were that special."

"Funny. Very funny." She dropped the rotten pizza into a big green garbage bag and flopped onto the spot she'd cleared on the sofa. "She turned forty years old today and is convinced she'll die before her forty-first birthday because most of her blood relatives on her father's side of the family did."

"So?"

"She wants to put me, I mean us, on retainer for $5,000 a month to find homes for all of her pets."

"FIVE THOUSAND DOLLARS A MONTH?"

Baye held the phone away from her ear when Libby shouted the number. "She has stipulations, though, and wants to negotiate a contract that we both sign to make sure her wishes are carried out."

"How many months is she planning to do this? What if she turns forty-one and hasn't died?" Libby's words came out in a rush. "Shit, just one month would let us pay off the vet, hire some part-time kennel help, and maybe sock some savings away."

"I guess that would depend on how long it takes us to find good homes for her animals."

Libby slowed her babble only a little. "How many does she have? She could just sell the sheep, goats, and llama that are in the pasture next to us. I don't know about the donkey. Who would want a loud-mouthed donkey?"

"She doesn't want the sheep and goats sold to someone who might sell them for slaughter. They're pets. She also has a pot-bellied pig, chickens, rabbits, a huge parrot, a monkey, a Maine coon, and two dogs...correction, just the big white dog. The little terrier will go to her housekeeper."

"Okay. It could take months to find homes for the monkey, parrot, and raccoon, but them being so hard to place will be a good reason to take several months. That would let us clear our past-due accounts, and I could quit this waitressing job I hate."

Baye burst into laughter. "A Maine coon is a very large cat, not a raccoon."

"Whatever. What time should I be there? I'm flexible because I'm off work tomorrow...I mean today. It's stupid to even ask, but do you need help cleaning that garbage dump you live in?"

Baye looked over her shoulder at the kitchen. Dirty dishes and trash filled the sink and covered the countertops, not to mention the smell coming from the refrigerator. "Yeah. I'll text Teague in the morning and tell her to come over around three o'clock."

"That sounds good. Now let me get some sleep, and I'll be there no later than eight in the morning."

"Bring doughnuts and coffee. Judging from the smell, I'm not sure we should eat anything out of this refrigerator."

Chapter Nine

"What the hell are you doing?" Libby stood just inside the front door, holding a cardboard tray and surveying the chaos of paint cans, brushes, two ladders, and computer paper scattered along the living room/dining room floor.

"Thank God you're here. I've been up all night, but I'm almost finished," Baye said. She felt euphoric after taking a couple of extra Adderall pills, an amphetamine medication prescribed for her ADHD, to stay awake. She'd take another to get through the day, too. She could crash for a long sleep tonight.

"This place is an even bigger mess than yesterday." Libby glared at her. "You're supposed to be cleaning. Why are you painting?"

"I hated that wallpaper even when I was a kid. Just the fact that it's been there for at least fifteen years is enough reason to remove it." Damn. Libby was always bringing her down.

"I don't disagree with that, but this is not the time to be remodeling, damn it." Libby looked at floor. "Is that my printing paper all over the floor?"

"I needed something to protect the floor from drips."

"Clearly it didn't." The pages had slipped this way and that as Baye had walked on them, leaving large portions of the floor unprotected and an apparent magnet for drips and spills. "That was an extra-large pack of printer paper I just bought yesterday, Baye. Did you use all of it?"

"I'll buy you lots more paper after Teague pops that first five thousand dollars in my bank account."

"You mean Heavy Petting's bank account."

Baye rolled her eyes. "Yes. In the business account."

Libby looked around. "If you haven't texted her yet about the meeting time, you probably should make it around five o'clock, rather than three. It'll take that long to get this place halfway clean, then for you to get showered. You stink of sweat and have paint in your hair."

"I texted her last night that we'd meet at three this afternoon." She stepped back to admire her work. She wasn't crazy about the blue color, but it was left over from the cathouse construction and all that was available in the middle of the night.

"We'll take ten minutes for coffee and doughnuts, and then we better get busy. I'll tackle the kitchen while you clean up in here."

Baye put down her paintbrush. "Yum. Doughnuts."

❖

"Get up! You have only twenty minutes to get yourself cleaned up."

Baye jerked awake when the recliner was nearly tipped over backward. She'd finally finished scrubbing the last of the paint from the hardwood floors and planned to sit down for only a minute. She scowled at Libby. "Shit. You nearly tipped me over." She rubbed her tired eyes. "What time is it?"

"Twenty minutes until three. I've cleaned up that awful kitchen and the stinky refrigerator. Then I cleaned the downstairs bathroom."

Baye stood and stretched. "Good. I'll shower in there. The one upstairs is nasty."

"Oh, no, you don't. You are not going to mess up the bathroom I just cleaned. If the upstairs one is nasty, it's your own dirt and soap scum."

"Okay, okay." She took a few seconds to collect herself. She'd meant to take another Adderall. "I'm going. If Teague gets here before I'm ready, just hang out with her. I'll be quick."

She took only a few steps when her phone quacked to indicate a new text message.

Teague: Just to clarify—you are coming here at three, right? I want your cousin to also meet my animals too before we review the contract.

She stared at the message. "Shit."

"What?" Libby peered over Baye's shoulder to read the text and growled. "I'm going to kill you."

"I'll tell her to come over here." She started to reply, but Libby snatched the phone from her and began typing.

"Get in the shower, damn it." She handed the phone to Baye so she could read the reply she sent.

Baye: I've been painting and was about to jump in the shower, so we might be a few minutes late.

The phone quacked again.

Teague: Okay. See you soon.

She smiled at Libby. "Guess I can use the clean bathroom since she's not coming here."

"Over my dead body," Libby growled through clenched teeth. "I didn't spend an hour cleaning that bathroom for you to trash it again so soon. Now go. Get. In. The. Shower."

"Okay, okay. You don't have to get huffy."

❖

Teague paced in front of the kitchen island and back, her agitation growing with each minute. Multiple copies of the contract were printed and ready for review. Connie had prepared finger sandwiches and bite-sized bakery sweets artfully displayed and covered in two glass cake stands to protect them from marauding parrots and monkeys. She looked at her phone again. Twenty minutes past three. Baye had said they would be a few minutes late. She fought the overwhelming urge to wait on the front porch. Connie had advised pacing the porch would look too anxious. But, damn, she couldn't stop thinking about the kiss the night before. Of course, she wouldn't expect a kiss like that today since Baye would have her cousin with her, but how should she greet her? The sound of doorbell chimes jerked her from her thoughts. "Walk, do not run to the door," she said to the empty room. So, she trotted.

"Hi. Sorry we're so late," Libby said when Teague opened the door.

"I was beginning to wonder if you changed your mind." Although her response was to Libby's apology, her eyes were on Baye as the implied question hung in the air between them—did she regret the kiss? To her relief, Baye's smile was soft as she stepped forward and placed a chaste kiss on Teague's cheek.

"It's my fault. I had to shampoo my hair three times to get all the paint out." Baye stepped closer and wrapped her in a long, tight hug to whisper in her ear. "Forgive me?"

All her doubts fled as Baye's hug dissolved the anxiety singing through her body. "Yes." She stepped back when Baye released her. "Please come inside." She led them to the formal dining room, where she intended to review the contract and negotiate any requested changes. Two copies were laid out, along with pens for any changes and a laptop where she could instantly make any agreed revisions and reprint for signatures or for their attorney's review.

Libby sat where Teague indicated, but Baye frowned and remained standing. "Can I say hello to the kids first?"

Teague was puzzled. "I do not have children."

"Your animal children, silly. You wanted Libby to meet them."

She thought this suggestion over. Meeting the animals before agreeing to a contract did make sense. What had she been thinking? She was thinking of that kiss. "You make an excellent point." She indicated the door that led to the open-concept kitchen and living area. "Mac and Cappie are in the sunroom."

Baye stopped at the kitchen island. "Oh my God. Connie made this for us?"

"Yes. Some of the small sandwiches are cucumber and cream cheese. Others have chicken-salad or shrimp-salad filling. The second cake stand contains bite-sized brownies, baklava, and cheesecake." She always needed to know what she was about to taste before she put it into her mouth and figured they would have the same requirement.

"This looks so good, and I'm starving. I haven't had anything to eat since early this morning."

"I apologize. I should have offered the food first." She shifted nervously from foot to foot, inwardly cursing herself for her social ineptness. "We have bottled water, lemonade, and sun tea to drink."

"It's fine," Libby said. "I vote for business first…to get it out of the way." She elbowed her cousin. "Quit acting like a feral stray."

"Ow. Oka-ay. Geez. I'll just grab a few of these little sandwiches for now," Baye said as she loaded one of the dessert plates Connie had set out on the counter. "We can eat the rest later."

"Pretty, Pretty," Mac screamed from the sunroom, then sang, "You are my sunshine."

Cappie spotted them and chattered as he ran back and forth along the top of his cage.

"Mac! Cappie!" Baye picked up her plate and went into the sunroom.

"You are my sunshine," Mac sang again. He fluttered down from his cage and walked over when Baye knelt to greet him. "Treat. Mac wants a treat."

She looked up at Teague. "Is it okay to share with him?"

Teague was pleased that she was so engaged with her pets.

"They love cucumber, but the cream cheese will upset their stomachs. Connie said they would beg, so she left some cucumber slices in the refrigerator. I will get them."

Cappie scrambled down his cage to sit alongside Mac when Baye sat cross-legged on the floor. "How are you guys doing?" she asked.

"How are you?" Mac said, while Cappie fingered her ankle bracelet. Mac noticed Cappie's interest in the bracelet and moved to hold it in his beak and explore it with his tongue.

Libby laughed. "Does he know what he's saying?" She sat on the floor next to Baye. "That's a huge beak. I'll bet he could totally bite your finger off."

"No biting. Biting bad. Bad Mac bite."

"That is right, Mac. Biting is bad," Teague said as she returned and handed a plastic container of cucumber slices to Baye.

"Treat!" Mac's scream made Baye and Libby startle, but he was very gentle as he took a cucumber slice from Baye's hand. Cappie's grab for his treat was lightning quick. Mac politely nibbled his slice, while Cappie chowed down on his.

"You can give them the next slice," Baye said, handing the container to Libby. Like Cappie, she chowed down on the finger sandwiches on her plate.

Even Teague winced when an ear-splitting squeal sounded in the yard. Flower had spied them and probably smelled the cucumber. Judging from the mud covering her, she'd had a roll at the pond's edge and was running across the yard to join them. Cappie snatched a second slice from the container Libby had in her lap, climbed the side of his cage until he could reach one of the ropes that hung from the ceiling, and used it to swing over and settle on Teague's shoulder.

"Flower's coming." Baye looked up at Teague with a warm smile.

Teague offered a hand to help her stand, and Baye, in turn, pulled Libby up from the floor. "Pigs have a very good sense of smell, and cucumbers are one of her favorite foods. We should meet her outside. The cleaning staff mopped this floor this morning."

They met Flower on the terrace but stood back while Teague washed the black mud from her.

Libby shoved the cucumber container into Baye's hands. "I'm not sure about feeding a pig. I've seen movies where they ate people."

Teague frowned. "Flower will not bite or eat people. She is not a wild pig." She decided to demonstrate and held up a slice for Flower to see. "Sit, Flower."

Flower grunted but obediently sat on her haunches and was rewarded with the treat.

She made a twirling motion with her fingers, and Flower spun in a circle to earn a second one. She was pleased when Baye and Libby applauded the trick. Now for the grand finale. "This is the trick I like best and was the easiest to teach her." She held up the last cucumber slice. "Tongue," she said, sticking out her own tongue in demonstration. Flower immediately stuck out her own tongue and waved it at them. Teague grinned when Baye and Libby laughed and clapped at Flower's antics. This was going well.

"Do we have time to go down to the barn?" Baye asked. "I want Libby to see the rest of your brood."

"Yes." She almost stumbled when Baye linked their arms together for the walk, but her chest seemed to swell with something unexpected. Pride? Comfort? Affection? She didn't know which, but it felt good. Very good.

❖

Teague put the contract down. "You can have your attorney go over the small print before you sign, but let me summarize the main points. I must approve any potential home you find. No zoos or petting zoos. Those places are stressful for the animals.

Lucky and Snow need a herd to work. Cappie is a good candidate to be trained as a support animal for someone paralyzed.

"Mac will be hard to place. He knows enough bad words that he must be placed with an experienced bird person with no young children. The sheep, goats, rabbits, and chickens must be allowed to live out their lives and never sent to slaughter. Their adoption contracts will include a stiff financial penalty if this stipulation is violated."

"What about Flower? Oh, and Asset?" They had moved to the den/kitchen area, where they ate the rest of the snacks and worked around a coffee table so Mac, Cappie, Leo, and Flower could join them.

"I would like a home with another pet pig for Flower. Pigs are herd animals and very social within their species. Before I learned that my odds of living past forty-one were slim, I had planned to find a pig friend for her." She frowned. "I don't have a clear picture of where Asset might thrive other than here. His mother died having him, and he was bottle-raised so is more oriented toward people than other animals. He would rather look in a window to watch people than spend time guarding a herd. You and I will have to figure out the best situation for him."

"So, do you have a timeline?" Libby asked. "Baye said you are offering five thousand dollars a month to find homes for them. How many months do you anticipate?"

"Twelve months. If something happens to me before the twelve months is up, my lawyer will still transfer the money into your account each month."

"What if we secure homes for them in one or two months?"

"I don't think you'll be able to, but the contract states that after placement, you will check their new homes monthly to make sure my animals are thriving there."

Libby picked up her pen. "Where do we sign?"

Teague was taken aback that Libby didn't consult with Baye, who was untangling her hair that Cappie had burrowed into. "Baye? Do you agree?"

"I would have signed the minute we walked in the front door. I trust you."

"Please have your lawyer look it over. You can sign now but have three days to nullify the contract if you want." She would never sign a contract without vetting it first and was dismayed that Baye consented so easily.

Baye made a face and held Cappie out in front of her. "I think he needs a diaper change."

Teague took the monkey from her, went to the changing table tucked into the corner of the room, and quickly corrected the stinky situation. Libby looked a little green when she returned to her guests.

"Are you feeling okay?" Teague asked.

Libby pulled the neck of her T-shirt over her mouth and nose. "His poop really stinks."

"She gags when she has to change a baby's stinky diaper," Baye said cheerfully. The odor apparently didn't affect her.

"Oddly enough, I cannot tolerate perfumes, but manure does not bother me," Teague said.

"That is odd." Libby's words were muffled by the shirt still covering her mouth. She signed the contract quickly, handed it to Baye to sign, and then held out a folded paper to Teague. "This is the rescue center's banking information for an electronic transfer."

"I'll move the money over tonight," she said.

"Thank you." Libby stood. "Ready, Baye?"

"I was about to offer you coffee on the terrace," Teague said. Connie had helped her make a step-by-step list of how to entertain her guests. They would review the contract, eat the snacks, visit the animals, then have coffee last. Introducing Libby to the animals before reviewing the contract had agitated her at first, but she did see the logic of it, and having Baye's arm linked in hers as they walked to the barn had instantly settled her frustration.

"That sounds great," Baye said, then looked to Libby. "You

go ahead. I'll walk home across the pasture in a little bit," she said, taking another brownie and popping it into her mouth.

Libby was already trying to unlock the decorative wrought-iron door that kept the animals from the rest of the house, so Teague opened it for her.

"Thanks," Libby said as she waved over her shoulder. "I can see myself out."

The front door opened, then closed as Libby escaped, and Teague turned back to Baye. "She does not like animals?"

"Not like you and I do," Baye said. "Grandma left the farm to both of us so Libby could handle the finances and, well, my finances. Having very little impulse control is part of having ADHD. I have difficulty managing money."

Teague needed to read more about ADHD. She sat on the sofa next to Baye. "Can you give me an example?"

Baye's face flushed pink. "Sometimes I spend money on unnecessary things like a new cat tree, forgetting the light bill needs to be paid instead. I'm not proud of it. I just have trouble controlling my impulse unless someone is in my ear, like Libby, reminding me I have to pay it."

"So, Libby makes sure the mortgage and utilities are taken care of?" An adult being unable to manage their household bills puzzled her.

"And the animals are fed and their medical needs met. Grandma left a trust that pays for upkeep on the farm, taxes, and insurance. She knew we wanted to start a rescue center, so she designated money to start up Heavy Petting, and the trust allots so much a month for operating expenses. Neither of us anticipated the volume of animals that needed rescuing, and the monthly trust allotment barely covers food for them."

"What is your role at the rescue?"

Baye brightened. "Oh, I built the website and handle marketing, adoptions, and help John clean the kennels and cathouse." She paused. "Well, I'm supposed to help. I forget sometimes when something else distracts me. I'm good at marketing and creative stuff."

Teague turned this information over in her mind. "What would help you?"

"This contract, your money will help a lot. We can pay off our debt to our veterinarian. Libby can quit her waitressing job and work full time at the rescue. And we may be able to hire some part-time help."

"Yes. I have asked Bruce to see if another veterinary student might be interested in the job." Teague shook her head. "But I meant to say, how can I help you? I am fortunate enough to have the resources to build an environment around myself that helps me deal with my disability. Now, I want to help you."

Baye's expression was pained. She looked down at her hands clasped in her lap. "You don't want to get involved with me, Teague. A lot of people have tried, but ultimately, they give up on me and walk away."

"What I do is my decision." She took Baye's hands in hers. "I do not have friends. I have only Connie and Aunt Margaret, and maybe Mary Anne. Yet I have been comfortable with you since the day we met." She stared down at their linked hands and whispered her confession. "I may want to be more than friends." Heat flushed her chest and neck. "I liked our kiss last night."

"I did, too. Very much," Baye said just as quietly. "I'm just afraid I will do something to let you down or drive you away."

She glanced, trying to hold Baye's gaze for a long second. "I am afraid I will not have time enough to explore our connection. I do not like people to touch me, yet I want to touch you and let you touch me every minute I am with you. I want to kiss you again."

Baye's expression turned from pained to delighted. "I want to kiss you, too." And she did.

The kiss was soft at first, then hungry—Baye's lips were so soft, her tongue was warm, and her mouth tasted of the peppermint-bark candy she'd just eaten. Warmth spread throughout Teague, her lower belly did a slow roll that would have bucked her hips if she'd been lying down, and her heart pounded in her ears. Her heart. She jerked back, her hand on her chest.

Baye's eyes were wide, and she placed her hand over Teague's chest. "Are you all right?"

"My heart is pounding. It might burst." She began to hyperventilate. Her breaths quickened, but her lungs were still starved.

Baye cupped Teague's face in her hands. "Deep breath. Close your eyes and take a deep breath. Good. Another. And another."

Her heart began to slow, and the tightness squeezing her lungs lessened. She was sweating, but she could breathe again. She opened her eyes. "I think I am okay."

Baye smiled. "Oh, honey. My heart was beating hard and fast, too. It was the kiss."

She frowned. "I know about arousal. I am not a forty-year-old virgin."

"Yes. You said you dated other women. But when you have real feelings for someone, everything is so much more—kissing, touching, sex. Have you had feelings for another woman or a man before?"

She thought this over. "No. My brain does not process emotions."

Baye shook her head. "Who told you that? I've seen you angry, and I've seen you display affection for your animals. You obviously love Connie, and I can feel the bond developing between us. Those are all emotions."

She was doubtful. "My parents said I was diagnosed as a child. They were told my aversion to being touched was because I was autistic and did not feel emotion."

"Those doctors were either wrong, or you've progressed as you grew older."

"I still do not like for anyone to touch me."

"Really? I've seen you let Connie hug you and Cappie

groom your hair." Baye moved to sit in her lap. "How do you feel when I touch you?"

She reflexively wrapped her arms loosely around Baye's waist. "I told you. I like it when you touch me. I like touching you, too."

That tingling sensation started again as Baye kissed her neck, and her heartbeat quickened. "My heart—" She again pressed her hand to her chest and stood so fast, Baye fell unceremoniously onto the floor. Teague scrambled to help her stand. "I am very sorry. My heart was beating too fast again."

Baye only laughed. "Okay. I get the message." She let Teague help her up from the floor. "No heavy kissing or petting until your MRI. When is it scheduled?"

"I am not sure. There is a high demand in this area, and mine is preventative rather than diagnostic, so it is a low priority."

"Will they give you the results right away?"

"Normally, they do not. However, I am paying for this outside insurance, and my parents made substantial donations to the children's wing, so a neurologist and cardiologist may be present to immediately read the results."

"I want to go with you."

Teague was surprised. "You cannot go into the MRI room with me. You would have to sit in a waiting room."

"Can I be with you when they tell you the results?"

Teague considered this request. "Yes. I suppose you can."

"Then I'd like to go with you."

She started to refuse, but the confines of the MRI machine were stressful. Perhaps Baye's presence would calm her. "I think I would like that."

Baye touched her cheek. "Good. Now how about walking me home?"

"Will there be more kissing?"

"Just a peck. I promise."

"Okay, then."

CHAPTER TEN

I can't believe you're still asleep. Get up. It's one o'clock in the afternoon." Libby hit Baye in the face with one of the small decorative pillows.

"Ow." Baye rubbed her eyes, then glared at her cousin. "I was up almost all night looking for chat groups or social media posts involving parrots or pigs. I'm trying to find possible homes for Mac and Flower."

Libby looked skeptical. "Really?"

"Check my web history if you want." She was feeling grumpy from lack of sleep and very little progress. She sat up and rubbed her eyes again. She really shouldn't take it out on Libby. She deserved Libby's distrust, given her history of abusing her Adderall prescription, then crashing for a day or even two. "I'm sorry. I'm really trying hard to help Teague."

Libby, chewing her lower lip, stared at her. "No. I'm sorry. You like her a lot, don't you?"

Baye slumped against the sofa's cushioned arm. "We have a connection I can't explain. Maybe it's because neither of us is perfect. We both struggle in a world that says we're not normal." She finally smiled. "And, damn, she's a great kisser."

Libby's answering smile was soft. "I hope it works out for you, cuz. You're different around her...more settled. And you deserve some peace in your life."

Baye stood and hugged her. "Thank you. I know sticking

by me hasn't been easy for you." She paused when her throat tightened. "I love you."

"Stop. You're going to make me cry," Libby said. "Although you're exasperating sometimes, I do love you."

"Did you bring food for me?" She eyed the tray Libby had placed on the coffee table before rudely waking her. It held a bag from their favorite burger joint and two sodas.

Libby released her with a laugh. "You know I did because you never have anything to eat in this house."

"Yum." She grabbed the bag and dug out a cheeseburger, unwrapped it, and took a huge bite before reaching back in for a serving of French fries.

"I have news." Libby retrieved her burger and fries in a less ravenous manner. "The money showed up in our account yesterday, but when I called Dr. Jayne to pay off our vet bill, her receptionist said someone had already paid it off."

Baye shook her head. "It had to be Teague. I told her we planned to use some of the five thousand to pay our vet." She munched a couple of fries. "Did you quit your job?"

"I gave notice. I hate the job, but my boss is really nice, so I didn't want to walk out before she has a chance to hire someone in my place. That shouldn't take long, considering that college students are always looking for a part-time job."

"Great. Teague's part-time guy is going to send me the name of a fellow vet student to clean kennels for us."

"Good. Because I am not cleaning kennels. I can take over the adoption applications from you and handle the finances. You can work on the Teague project, do the event planning, keep the website updated, and oversee enrichment activities for the cats and dogs."

Baye nodded. She hated paperwork but loved anything that involved direct contact with the animals and social media or web related. "That sounds good. In fact, I think I'll go visit our furry friends now. I have a surprise for the dogs."

❖

"I have to fill up these pups' water bowl several times each day," John said.

Teague studied the kennel and the elderly man, his back bent with arthritis, who dragged over a long, heavy hose to fill the bowl in a kennel that held four very young Labrador-mix puppies. Their water bowl was large and built so it wouldn't easily tip over. "If they are drinking that much, maybe they have a medical problem. Where is their mother?"

"Hit by a car and killed. A good Samaritan saw her body in the road, and when he got out to move her to the side so cars wouldn't keep running over her, he noticed she had full teats and found the litter of puppies nearby in the woods. He's a student and didn't have a place to keep them, so he brought them here. Luckily, they were old enough to wean."

Teague frowned. "And your vet has checked them out? One or more of them could be diabetic if they are drinking a lot of water."

"Oh, yes. Baye's in charge of intake. She makes sure Dr. Jayne sees any new animals. It's not that they drink too much. They play in the water and slosh it out of the bowl."

She thought about offering to take them to her pond for a romp, but it might be dangerous for pups that young. They needed a wading pool. For that matter, she could design automatic waterers so John wouldn't have to drag that heavy hose down the long hallway that had kennels on both sides.

John took down a leash hanging on the door to the run that contained a large, overweight pit bull. "Time for this one to get some exercise. You might want to stand back. Buster's friendly but hates being confined. Sometimes, I can't hold on to him when he rushes to the play yard."

"Please, let me take him for you."

"Are you sure? He's really strong and has pulled me down several times."

"Yes. I can handle him." She looped the slip-leash around his nose and neck. Buster started to bolt toward the fenced play yard, but the leash tugged at his chin, rather than his muscular neck, and he stopped. "Good boy," Teague said, rewarding him with a pat on the head before walking him to one of three twenty-by-forty-yard fenced areas. His tail whipped back and forth as he bounced on his front feet, but he stopped pulling after several tries. He stood quietly when she opened the gate, then sprinted away when she released him from the leash.

They were watching him run, jump into the air, and joyfully roll in the grass when Baye called out to them. She was dragging a six-foot-round plastic child's wading pool toward them.

"Teague. Hey. I didn't know you were coming over. You should have texted me," she said.

Teague turned, and her belly did a little flip at Baye's wide smile. "I did text this morning, but you did not reply. I came to tell you I have found some kennel help for you. Bruce will bring him here at two o'clock." She glanced at her watch. "In ten minutes."

"Oh. I'm so sorry. I was up until six this morning scanning social media sites and the web for people who might provide good homes for your pets. I fell asleep around seven, and Libby woke me up only an hour ago. I didn't see your message." She dropped the pool and entwined her fingers with Teague's to tug her close and buss her on the cheek. "At any rate, I'm very pleased to see you."

The warmth that suffused Teague was becoming familiar now. It happened every time she was near Baye. "I am pleased to see you, too," she said.

"So, is that for the dogs?" John asked, pointing to the pool.

"Yes, it is," Baye said. "Since the days are getting warmer, I thought they might like some water fun." She went back to the pool. "Can you guys pitch this over the fence while I get the hose?"

Teague and John picked up the lightweight pool and tossed it where Baye had pointed, then went through the gate to position it.

"How far does the hose reach?" Teague asked John as they set it on a thick patch of grass.

"An outdoor spigot is right over there by the last play yard," he said, pointing.

John filled the pool while Teague and Baye retrieved the four Labrador puppies that had gone into the indoor part of their kennel.

"How's your heart today?" Baye asked, taking her hand again as they entered the pups' kennel.

"My heart is good." The question surprised her.

"Let's see." Baye pressed Teague against the concrete wall while the puppies jumped against their legs to be petted. She wrapped her hand firmly around Teague's nape and guided her down for a long, deep kiss.

She reflexively wrapped her arms around Baye and pressed their hips together. Baye finally pulled back and patted Teague's chest. "I think we should do that occasionally to exercise that organ you think might be weak."

Teague laid her hand over Baye's and held it to her wildly beating heart. "You will either kill me or make it stronger, but I am thinking it may be worth the risk."

Baye grinned. "Let's go see if the puppies like their new pool."

❖

The pool was an instant hit with the puppies, who splashed and wrestled in the water. John chuckled at their antics, and Buster, in the adjoining play yard, whined and ran in circles.

"He wants to join them." The voice that sounded behind them was deep, but somehow contained a childlike quality.

Baye turned to see Bruce and a mountain of a man with a bushy beard standing at the fence.

Bruce waved. "Hi. The lady in the house said to come on back."

Baye smiled. "That's my cousin, Libby. She co-owns this place with me." She walked over to the fence and realized the man was younger than he appeared at a distance. She held out her hand. "Hi. I'm Baye."

"Go ahead. Shake her hand and tell her your name. She's very nice," Bruce prompted the man.

He was gentle as he briefly clasped her hand. "My name is Tommy. I want to help take care of your dogs."

While his appearance was a little intimidating, he was obviously mentally handicapped and a little shy. Baye instantly liked him. "Hi, Tommy. We have cats, too."

"I love kitties." His face lit up like she'd said Santa Claus was in the cathouse. He pointed to the puppies frolicking in the pool. "I love puppies, too."

"We'll have to show them to you," Baye said. John and Teague joined them. "Tommy, this is my neighbor, Teague, and this is John. He's our gardener but helps with the animals, too."

He nodded but wrung his hands together rather than offer a handshake. "Nice to meet you, Miss Teague and Mr. John." His gaze wandered to Buster, who was watching the puppies and jumping up and down. "He wants to play in the pool, too. Can I go pet him?"

"Sure. John, can you get the gate for him?" Baye watched Tommy follow John to the other yard.

Teague stared after him. "Bruce?"

"I know he might look a little rough, but he's kind and gentle and a very hard worker."

"How do you know him?" Baye asked.

"He's been working at the vet school cleaning, feeding,

exercising animals, and anything else they need him to do. He is also very strong, as you can tell by his size, so they would call him in to the clinic if they needed someone to hold the large dogs to doctor them. He especially loves pit bulls and has a sixth sense when it comes to knowing if they're friendly, scared, or dangerous."

They all turned to see him sitting on the ground and letting Buster lick his face while John stood nearby.

"Here's the thing. He lives in a group home near the vet school and walks to work. But the school is renovating their clinic and kennels. They'll operate in a smaller, rented building for the next year but will greatly decrease their client numbers so the students can manage the reduced workload. Short story is they laid him off. He's been working there almost ten years and is devastated."

"Poor Tommy." Baye's heart hurt for him. "Does he have family who'll take him in?"

Bruce shook his head. "His parents had him very late in life and have passed away. The vet school was his whole existence. He doesn't like the group home because they have fights there and the other men sometimes bully him. Even with his size and strength, he'll crumple into a ball and cry before he'll hit anyone. He's still living there because he's not capable of being on his own. He doesn't know how to cook or wash clothes and has to be told to shower. I was going to take him to a barber and get him cleaned up before I brought him over here, but I was afraid you'd give the job to someone else if I took time to do that."

John joined them. "Tommy says Buster wants to play with the puppies and won't hurt them." He turned to Bruce. "If Buster does go after one of the puppies, or if a dog fight broke out between two of the big dogs, would he be able to step in and break it up, or would he panic?"

"Like I said, he's very strong and has been taught how to break up a dog fight. He's shy with people but very commanding with the animals...like they're his children." Bruce turned and shouted at Tommy. "Go ahead. Buster's leash is hanging on the gate."

John nodded and looked to Baye and Teague. "I like him. My wife and I had a son with Down syndrome. He was twenty-eight when he was killed in the same car wreck that took my Martha. How about we hire Tommy on a trial basis? I've got two bedrooms in my cottage. He can stay with me." He pointed to the small house on the edge of the woods behind the kennels. "I'm not getting any younger, and he could help me."

"Are you sure, John?" Baye asked. "Taking him into your home is asking a lot."

John nodded. "I've been lonely for years without Martha and Kenny. My daughter lives five hours away, and I don't want to live with her family. They are too busy, and I'd feel useless there. This farm has been my home for most of my adult life, and I'd welcome the company."

"Baye is only looking for part-time help," Teague pointed out. She squinted, rubbed her temples, and moved so the sun was at her back.

"We could maybe pay him less than we were going to offer, since he'll be getting room and board," Baye said, warming to the idea. "John can manage his money for him and keep some to pay for his groceries."

Bruce cleared his throat. "Uh, this only came up today when they told us about the vet-school renovations. They're farming out the senior students—those of us who've reached the clinical part of our training—to other vet schools or big clinics. I'm being sent to Raleigh in August to finish my education at the North Carolina State vet school." He looked to Teague. "I think Tommy could handle your place and this one when I'm gone."

Baye was unsure how Teague would respond, given her ridiculous notion that she was going to die before her next birthday, and was surprised when Teague nodded.

"The animals and I will miss you. You have been a good

worker," Teague told Bruce. "I trust your recommendation since you have worked with Tommy at the university."

"Look!" Tommy called to them. "Look at Buster." The big dog was lying in the middle of the wading pool while the puppies crawled all over him. One puppy was trying to catch Buster's tail as it wagged and splashed in the water. The big dog licked each one's head in turn.

Bruce laughed. "You might have found a good puppysitter."

"Looks that way," John said, chuckling at the dogs' antics. "I think that old dog might have been lonely, too."

"Tommy is definitely hired," Baye said, laughing along with John and Bruce. She instantly liked the big man-child and could see that John did, too.

"On a thirty-day trial," Teague reminded her, rubbing her forehead.

"Okay," Baye said. "But I'm betting he's a perfect fit for Heavy Petting."

"I will leave it to you and John to work out when he can come over for you to teach him how to care for my animals," Teague said to Bruce. "You should start by putting a gate in the fence on this side of the pasture so he can walk back and forth."

Baye's heart swelled at this immediate kindness from her outwardly stoic girlfriend, and she applauded the decision. Wait. Girlfriend? Her heart did a happy dance. Yes. She just hoped Teague felt the same way.

They left John and Bruce to show Tommy the ropes and take him to Libby so she could fill out the employment paperwork.

"Are you okay?" Baye kept her voice soft. "You keep rubbing your forehead."

Teague closed her eyes and squeezed the bridge of her nose. "I wanted to go over some of the adoption contracts I have completed, but I woke up with a headache that is getting worse. I think I should go home and lie down."

Baye's heart skipped a beat. Had Teague been right about

the family curse? "Maybe we should go see your doctor." She took off her sunglasses and placed them on Teague's face.

Teague heaved a sigh. "Thank you." She shook her head carefully. "No doctor. This is a sinus headache because a storm is expected later today."

"Then let me go home with you. If it gets worse, you'll need someone to drive you to a doctor or the emergency room." She gripped Teague's hand when she started to protest. "You need a cup of hot tea, then to lie down in a dark room. Do you have something to take for your sinuses?"

Teague gave another cautious shake of her head.

She was careful to speak softly. "We have some Tylenol sinus pills because Libby gets those headaches, too, when it rains. I don't see your car, so I'm guessing you walked over."

"Yes." Teague's answer was almost a whisper.

"Okay. I'll grab the medicine from the house, then drive you home." She cupped Teague's elbow and guided her toward the farmhouse.

❖

Teague sank into the cool dark of her bedroom. The hot ginger tea Connie had made for her helped a little, and the pills were beginning to ease the throbbing in her face. Now, she lay on her back with a super-soft throw blanket covering her. Connie had helped her through these headaches before, but her new nurse was so much better. The weight and warmth of the body lying next to her after a gentle head-and-neck massage was draining the pain and the tension from her entire body.

"Is this okay?" Baye whispered into the dark as she entwined their fingers.

"Yes." She felt groggy, like she was floating after Baye's massage. She'd manipulated a pressure point just above the hairline that helped open swollen sinuses, and to Teague's surprise, it really worked. "Stay?"

"Yes, unless my being in your room keeps you from relaxing enough to sleep."

"Mmm." Her mouth felt dry and her head foggy. She tightened her fingers around Baye's. "I like you here."

"Then this is where I'll be when you wake up—tonight or tomorrow. I'll be here."

"Soon, there might not be a tomorrow for me, Baye." She closed her eyes and finally allowed sleep to take her.

Chapter Eleven

This place is disgusting." Libby gathered mail scattered in different places around the downstairs and shoved it into her messenger bag. "You're unreal. This is why you can't keep a roommate, and why I can't live here with you in a house that's half mine." She picked up a stack of mail from the living room coffee table and uncovered a plate of half-eaten Chinese takeout beginning to grow fuzz. "You are so gross. I'm taking this mail back to my apartment. I can't work in this stinking chaos until you clean it up."

"I don't have time. I'm going with Teague to get her MRI."

"I hope you're picking her up, because if she sees how you live, we're going to lose that contract. And right now, that's the only thing keeping Heavy Petting in the black." She picked her way through the debris of takeout cartons and discarded clothes to the front door. "I can't run this rescue and take care of you, too, Baye."

"It'd be easier if you moved back in here." Baye popped a peppermint into her mouth. It pretty much drowned out the smell.

"You mean it'd be easier for you because I'd spend half my time cleaning up your messes. It's a good thing Grandma left us this house, because you can be so disgusting, white trash with a yard full of beer cans and cigarette butts wouldn't even let you live in their neighborhood. You need help, and I'm tired of begging you to get some." Libby slammed the door behind her and drove off in a cloud of dust.

Baye could feel her meltdown building. She stomped around the room, kicking at the debris of dirty clothing, pizza boxes, and discarded shoes while chanting a long string of inventive curses. "Like she's Miss Perfect." She opened the back door and the front door to air out the smell, then sat down on the sofa after moving another greasy pizza box with a dark fungus growing inside.

Her agitation wasn't just about Libby's criticism. She hadn't seen Teague for almost a week. When she tried calling, Connie answered Teague's phone, explaining she was holed up in the cottage working on some new project and never took her phone there when she didn't want to be interrupted. Baye had waited three days before she marched across the pasture—through the new gate Bruce and Tommy had installed—and knocked on the cottage door before opening it.

"Anybody home?" She could see Teague was indeed there, a plate of uneaten food on the desk and Teague rapidly writing on the whiteboard while intermittently turning to adjust something on the contraption that covered most of her desk. She looked like she hadn't slept or bathed in several days. "Hey, you. Did Connie tell you I've been calling?"

Teague didn't look up or answer. She kept writing numbers on the whiteboard, mumbling as the equation grew longer. She turned toward the desk and pulled a pair of weird goggles down from the top of her head to cover her eyes and finally looked at Baye.

"You can't be in here. The laser will hurt your eyes." She came around the desk and pushed Baye toward the door. "Out, out," she said, closing and locking the door once Baye was outside.

Baye was shocked and turned to bang on the door but stopped when she realized Teague had pulled a heavy shade over the door's glass panes. Only then did she realize none of the animals were with Teague. Because of the laser?

So, Baye went home, rolled a bag of marijuana into joints, and ordered takeout to be delivered. Three more days had passed without a word, much less an apology, from Teague. She obviously was just a business contract to her, not a girlfriend.

She started to cry—an angry cry, not sad. "Nobody understands me," she screamed into the room.

She wiped away her tears when she heard Tommy noisily shuffling up the back steps with a bucket and mop.

"Miss Baye, is it okay to come in?"

Baye's anger drained away, and her control started returning with his tentative request. She would not be mean to Tommy because he also suffered a handicap that undoubtedly had made him a target of bullies in the past. "Please come on in, Tommy." She could tell John had already taken him under his wing. His features were a bit coarse and his expressions childlike, but he wasn't bad looking. "John took you to the barber shop, didn't he? Your haircut and beard look very nice."

He lowered his eyes, and his face flushed red. "Thank you, Miss Baye." His eyes went wide as he scanned the downstairs, then looked at a corner in the dining room where a puppy she'd brought up to the house had relieved himself. "Did you have a party here? I can clean up the dog stuff now and come back later to help you. John told me to go to Miss T's when I finish this."

"Don't worry about it," she said. "Have you seen Teague since the day we hired you?"

"Miss Connie said she was very busy working, but she better get done soon because the animals are missing her." His face transformed into wonder. "She has a monkey and a big, big parrot."

She couldn't help but smile at him. "And a pig."

"Yes! I like Flower. Miss T says Flower paints pictures, and I can watch her do it sometime."

"I'd like to see that, too." Baye sighed and went into the walk-in pantry to hunt for garbage bags. She might as well clean this up so Libby would come back and work at the house. Even though they argued endlessly, neither had any close friends, and their mutual loneliness always drew them back together. Her pantry search fruitless, she knelt to look through the cleaning products under the sink. Damn. She'd have to walk down to the kennels and get a new roll of bags.

"Miss T! You're here!"

Baye froze. Shit. Teague was going to see the mess. She silently berated herself for not cleaning earlier. She peeked around the doorless arch between the kitchen and dining room. She couldn't avoid Teague, who could see the open arches at either end of the kitchen from the front door where she was standing. Maybe she could hide in the pantry.

"Miss Baye was asking about you, and here you are," Tommy said. "She's in the kitchen."

Shit. So much for hiding.

"What happened here? Did someone break in and vandalize this house?"

Baye winced at the alarm in her question, then decided she should go ahead and face Teague's scrutiny. Anyway, how could Teague criticize her after rudely throwing her out of the cottage?

She stepped out from the kitchen. "Nobody broke in. I'm the vandal." She turned to Tommy. "Go check on the animals next door when you finish mopping, please. I'll clean up the rest here."

"Yes, ma'am. I like Cappie and Mac."

"Their pens are still clean after your visit early this morning, but I have not had much time to spend with them lately. Take Cappie and Mac down to the barn like I showed you—Cappie on your shoulder and Mac on your arm—so they can have a change of scenery, and you can spend some playtime with all the animals."

"Okay, Miss T. I can play with them until John calls me." Tommy dug a cheap pay-in-advance phone from his pocket and held it up for them to see. "John gave me a phone," he said, "so he won't have to yell to find me. Anyway, I'm going with him to the store later to get dog food. His back hurts when he picks up the big bags, so I'm going to do that for him."

"Thank you, Tommy," Baye said. "I don't have to worry about him working too hard since you're here to help him."

"I like living with John. He helps me a lot, too."

"Good. That's good, Tommy." She turned back to Teague, who hadn't stepped more than two feet inside the open front door. She was haggard, her dark eyes dull and cheeks sallow. Was she sick? "Are you ready to go to the hospital for your MRI? Give me five minutes to change clothes." A quick PTA bath—pussy, tits, and armpits—with a washcloth and pulling her hair into a ponytail should make her presentable.

Teague shook her head as she backed out onto the porch. "Can we talk out here?"

❖

Teague was reeling at the chaos she'd seen in the house and had to get out. Her calm, her sanity depended on keeping order in her life. Her agitation had ratcheted up every minute she stood among the detritus. Did Baye always live like this, or was this an episode of some sort? Her stomach felt hollow from days of working and eating little. Her thoughts were swirling in a dizzy turmoil. She took a deep breath and propped against one of the porch's supports to wait for Baye to join her.

Baye stood in the doorway, separated by an emotional chasm that hadn't existed before.

"If you don't want me to go with you, just say it."

She shook her head again. The MRI appointment wasn't what she wanted to talk about. "It has to be rescheduled because of a series of emergency cases." She studied her feet, unable to even glance at Baye. "It is okay if you have decided not to go with me."

"I want to be with you, but after the way you treated me when I came to the cottage last week, I have to wonder if you still want me with you."

While Teague's differently wired brain was an asset when she was solving work problems, it constantly failed her when forming relationships with people. That brain was now seeing an alternate path to answering Baye's accusation. "Please explain why your house looks like a hazardous-waste site."

Baye scowled. "Libby just chewed me out. I don't need another critic to list everything that's wrong with me." She turned to go back into the house.

"Please. I am not judging. I want to understand."

Baye stopped and turned, her eyes boring into Teague's peripheral vision. After a moment, her face relaxed and her gaze turned to searching.

"I want to understand," Teague repeated.

Baye visibly swallowed and averted her gaze. "I don't know. Sometimes I struggle to do anything more than sit on the sofa and order food deliveries. I start to clean up, then get distracted and move on to something else before I'm even halfway done. It's like I don't even see it piling up because I can't stay focused. When the mess gets too big, I'm overwhelmed by it and don't know where to start cleaning. It's like I'm immobilized by it all." She slumped against the side of the house. "Nobody understands how I struggle."

Teague nodded. "I do understand, even though my struggle is different. You suffer from lack of focus, but I struggle with being too focused. I can't stop once I start working on a problem. I need almost complete order in my life. Everything must be put back on the shelf, all my clothes properly put away or left in the laundry hamper. If you were to lock me in your house right now, I would go mad trying to put everything in order. I would clean up the trash, wash all the dishes, and scrub the floors with a brush."

"That doesn't sound so bad." Baye smiled for the first time since Teague had arrived.

"But I would not be able to stop there. I would reorganize your closets and cabinets. I need uncluttered surfaces, so I would pack away any trinkets and knickknacks. I would not be able to stop until I had put fresh paint on your walls, ceilings, and trim. You have crown molding in your kitchen, but not in the living and dining rooms. That would irritate me until it was fixed."

"Feel free to get busy in there."

Teague shook her head. "Did you not notice the excessive organization in my bedroom closet? Or the absence of photographs or artwork on my walls?"

"I thought it was because you have a full-time housekeeper and didn't like art." She frowned. "My house could look like that, too, if I had someone cleaning up after me every day."

"You are missing my point. I would not be able to eat or sleep until I had cleaned and painted every room in your house. Every minute I stood among your disorder, I was a step closer to a meltdown." She knelt in front of Baye and took her hand in both of hers. "When you came to the cottage last week, I was in the middle of an obsessive episode. I could see the solution to the problem I had been contracted to solve but had to work out how to get to that solution. I could not break my concentration and stop to talk with you. I do not mean that I did not want to. I could not. That is my struggle."

Baye's eyes filled with tears. "What are we going to do with each other? We're so different, yet so alike."

"We are going to help each other, maybe with a professional to assist us."

Baye made a face. "I've tried therapists. They put me on a lot of drugs that made me feel funny. I didn't like it."

"I have never met another person whose company I wanted,

and I want you a great deal. I find that I want to touch you." She brushed her fingertips along Baye's cheek. "And, to my surprise, I like when you touch me." She closed her eyes as she took Baye's hand and held it against her own cheek. "I do not just tolerate but welcome your touch." She opened her eyes. "So, please, can we try together? It will be difficult, but I have analyzed the odds of success and think it is possible."

Baye's lips on hers were warm and soft and tasting of peppermint.

"Yes."

CHAPTER TWELVE

Pretty, pretty." Mac screeched as he half flew, half hopped toward them from the barn. "Bad dog. Bad dog."

Teague bent to let him climb onto her forearm. "Who is being bad, Mac?"

Normally laid back and quiet, Snow was barking deeply and persistently, accompanied by Badger's shrill yaps and Tommy's frantic shouts.

Baye grabbed Teague's other arm. "Something's wrong. Hurry."

Teague clasped Mac to her chest as they ran through the barn to discover Tommy, brandishing a pitchfork and shouting at a young black bear. Snow stood in front of Tommy, teeth bared as he barked at the bear, which was sitting on its haunches and unsuccessfully trying to swat Badger as he darted in and out from different directions. The bear roared when Badger landed a bite on its butt. Behind their line of defense, Abigail, along with her kids, Tater and Tot, was trying to escape, but they all kept falling down, then struggling to their feet after about fifteen seconds, only to fall over again. Asset brayed loudly, and Lucky whistled warnings as they stood guard over the sheep they had herded to a corner of the pasture.

"Baye, wait." Teague didn't have time to get the shotgun from the barn office. She put Mac down and sprinted after Baye and joined her in waving her arms and shouting. Only then did she see the radio collar around the bear's neck. The pandemonium was clearly too much for the bear, and it turned, went over the wood fence, and disappeared into the forest beyond.

Tommy threw down his pitchfork and ran to the goats, all of them collapsing as he reached them. "He hurt Abigail and her kids." Tears wet his face as he ran his hands over each one, and then, after a moment, they individually stood shakily.

Teague walked to him, careful not to trigger another fainting spell among the terrified goats. "Tommy, Tommy. They are okay. They are fainting goats and become paralyzed for a few seconds when something scares them. It is natural for them to do that. They are not hurt. They were just scared."

"They fainted because they were scared?" He wiped his nose on his sleeve.

"Yes. Is that a carrot I see sticking out of your pocket?"

"I was feeding the bunnies when Snow started barking, and then I saw the bear."

"You can feed it to Abigail and her kids to make them feel better."

His face brightened. "I'll do that. I'll feed them the carrot. It's a big one so they can share."

Baye walked up, holding Badger wrapped in her T-shirt and lowering her voice. "Badger's been hurt. When the bear was swiping at him, I think one of claws must have caught him on the side."

"Let me see." Teague kept her voice low, too, while sparing a glance to make sure Tommy was occupied with the goats. The wound was about four inches long, a clean slice through the skin and hypodermis. The muscle tissue underneath didn't appear to be harmed. "He needs stitches." Frantic monkey calls came from the barn. "Sounds like someone else needs to calm down, too."

"Oh, no! Is Badger hurt?" Tommy, who had been all smiles while he fed the carrot to his goat friends, shifted uneasily from foot to foot, his face screwing up like he might cry again.

"He has a boo-boo on his side, so we're going to ask his doctor to take a look at it," Baye said. "The bear's claw was probably dirty, and we don't want it to get infected."

"I tried to chase the bear away. I told Badger and Snow to leave it alone, but they wouldn't listen." Tommy's big chest hitched with a sob. "I'm sorry, Miss T. I really tried to stop them."

Baye rubbed a soothing hand up and down his back, and Badger licked his hand.

"He will be okay, Tommy. Badger and Snow were protecting you and the other animals. That is their job." Teague wished she could comfort him, too. Her aversion to touching other people held her back, so she offered verbal reassurances and let Baye do the touching. They were a good team. "You were very brave, too, and smart to take the pitchfork with you. But next time, let the dogs do their job. We do not want you to get hurt."

"That's right," Baye said. "All the other animals need you to take care of them."

The big man shook his head. "I can't do that. You can be mad at me if you want, but I can't watch them get hurt."

"You are a good man, Tommy," Teague said. "Come up to the barn, and I will give you some treats for the rest of them. They were scared, too, even though they did not faint."

Baye handed Badger to her and took Tommy's hand to encourage him to follow her. "Are you okay, Tommy? Were you scared?"

"No, ma'am. I didn't have time to be scared until after the bear was gone and my heart was beating fast."

When Teague led them into the barn, Cappie made a flying leap to Baye's shoulder, where he hid in her long, curly hair.

"Bad dog. Bad dog." Mac fluttered down from where he was hanging onto a lead line and grabbed Teague's pants leg to crawl up to her shoulder.

"That was not a dog," Tommy said. "It was a scary bear." Mac seemed to think over this new word, so he repeated it. "Scary bear."

"Bad dog," Mac said.

"Scary bear," Tommy said again. "Scary bear."

Teague handed Tommy a bucket and loaded him up with alfalfa cubes. "They all like these. Give Asset and Lucky two each. They did a good job guarding the sheep. Then give one each to the goats and the sheep." She went to the refrigerator in the feed room and retrieved a tasty hambone. "And give this to Snow."

"What about Badger? He bit the scary bear."

"We better wait to make sure the vet doesn't have to sedate him to stitch up his cut," Baye said. "He'll get lots of treats after the vet fixes his boo-boo."

"Okay." Tommy nodded, then walked back to the pasture with the bucket full of them.

Baye turned to Teague. "You don't think the bear will come back, do you?"

"No. From his size, I would estimate he is only about two years old and may be out on his own after just leaving his mother. He was looking for food, but I doubt he expected the resistance he met after climbing the fence. Young bears are easier to scare away. He had a tracking collar on, and that is a national forest beyond the pond. I will contact the local ranger and report it. They will probably hunt him, tranquilize him, and relocate him somewhere that is not close to people. I will bring the animals into the barn, just in case."

"I should call John and tell him what happened so he can be prepared if the bear shows up at the kennels. He might try to get in the feed room. We have a lot of dog food in there."

"That is a good idea."

❖

Connie looked up from the potatoes she was peeling. "Where's your shirt, young lady?"

Baye pointed to Teague, who was coming in behind her with

Badger in her arms and Mac on her shoulder. "There was a bear in the pasture trying to get to the goats and sheep, and Badger got injured when he bit it. He has a cut on his side, so I wrapped him in my T-shirt to stop the bleeding."

"Scary bear," Mac said for the first time.

Connie's eyes went wide. "Oh my God." She threw the bowl of potatoes into the sink, hastily washed her hands, then went to Teague. "How bad is it?"

"He will be fine, but I think he needs a few stitches."

"I'll call Dr. Jayne and tell her we're bringing him in," Connie said, pulling her phone from her apron pocket. She punched in the vet's number. "My poor, brave boy." She bent to kiss Badger's head. "Yes, hello. This is Connie at the Maxwell residence. A bear has injured Badger. Can you let Dr. Jayne know we're on our way to your clinic? We're ten minutes from you." She took him from Teague, and the terrier licked her face. "I'll hold him while you drive."

"I need to call the forest ranger and report the bear," Teague said.

"I'll drive her," Baye said. "Tommy can help you put the animals in the barn. Then will you guys go check on John? I'm afraid he'll get hurt if the bear shows up there."

"You aren't dressed, Baye," Connie said, carefully cradling Badger in her arms, tears filling her eyes as she kissed his head again.

Baye chuckled. "How about we all take a deep breath. Badger's injury isn't life-threatening." She looked to Teague. "This is a sports bra, Connie. If you walked in a gym, you'd see a lot of women working out in this and some shorts." She turned to Teague and began disengaging Cappie from her hair. "Can you loan me a T-shirt and take Cappie?"

"Yes. I will put them in their cages where they will feel safe." She handed some keys to Baye. "Take the Jeep. Connie likes that one."

Really? How many cars did Teague have?

❖

Four.

Connie led the way to the door that opened into a four-car garage, the back wall containing shelves built around several rolling tool chests and a mobile workbench.

"Wow." Baye saw Teague's motorcycle at the far end of the huge room, and the rest of the garage was filled with the Jeep Grand Cherokee, a Hummer, a Mustang Shelby GT500, and a 2023 Corvette Z06.

"She likes those ridiculous muscle cars and that thing that looks like an army vehicle. She bought the Jeep for me to drive," Connie said.

Baye opened the passenger door of the Jeep, helped Connie get seated since she had Badger in her arms with his head resting on her ample breast, and then climbed into the driver's seat. She wanted to examine all the bells and whistles of the luxurious interior but knew Connie was anxious to get Badger to the vet. "Here we go," she said, pushing the button to bring the engine to life.

❖

"Yes. It was a juvenile black bear, only he was not black. He was light brown and had a green tracking collar. I am certain. I know the difference in body shape. This was a young black bear." Teague listened to the ranger on the other end of her call. "No. I could not see the numbers on the collar or the ear tag or the sex. I was intent on saving my animals. It was not aggressive. I think it was just hungry. I have a donkey, a llama, and a Great Pyrenees mix that routinely guard my small flock of sheep and goats. I think it was more resistance than the bear expected. Also, my terrier joined in and bit it on the butt. I do not think the bear was injured, but my dog is at the vet getting stitched up. It is not a bad injury, mainly a deep scratch." She listened again. "Yes. We have warned our nearest neighbor. They run a dog-and-cat rescue. The bear might try to get in their feed room, where a lot of cat and dog food is stored." A long pause, and then she rattled off her address. "Thank you."

Tommy looked at her expectantly. "They won't hurt the bear, will they? I think you're right. He was just hungry." He brightened. "We could leave a bag of dog food in the woods for him to eat."

"No, Tommy. You should never feed wild bears. They will learn to be dependent on people and keep coming back. This is a young bear that needs to learn to hunt. If he associates people with food, then he can become dangerous, and the rangers would have to kill him."

Alarm showed on Tommy's face. "They won't kill him, will they?"

"No. The ranger said they have been looking for that bear because the battery went dead on its tracking collar. They will come tomorrow to track him, then shoot him with a tranquilizer dart to make him sleep. Then they will check to make sure he is not injured, put a new collar on him, and take him to a place where there are no people so he can live like a wild bear should."

"Good. That's good," he said. "I don't want the bear to get hurt."

She gave his back a quick pat, surprising herself. She had initiated touching another person that was not Baye. "I do not want him hurt either." She pointed to the pasture. "In case he does come back tonight, help me get the animals in the barn so they will be safe. Then we will go check on John."

Tommy smiled. "Okay, Miss T."

❖

All in the small, crowded waiting room looked up when Baye burst into Dr. Jayne's waiting room with Connie, still clutching Badger, right behind her. "We have Badger. We called ahead."

A female vet tech in dark blue scrubs stepped out of the hallway. "Right this way," she said. "Dr. Jayne is waiting for him."

The veterinarian was preparing a surgical tray. "Lay him on the table, and let's take a look."

Connie put Badger down, and Dr. Jayne carefully unwrapped the T-shirt.

"Oh. This doesn't look bad at all for a fight with a bear."

"Will he be okay?" Connie's voice shook a bit.

"From the looks of this, he'll be fine. I'm going to sedate him for the stitches because I need to wash the wound out really well and take X-rays to make sure he doesn't have any cracked ribs or internal injuries we can't see. We'll wake him up when we're done so you can take him home with an antibiotic and something for pain."

"You guys can wait out front," the vet tech said.

"I'm not leaving him," Connie said, arms crossed over her chest. Badger sat up and licked her arm, then growled at Dr. Jayne's poking and prodding. "It's okay, my brave little man. Dr. Jayne is going to fix you up so you can go home."

Dr. Jayne turned to her assistant. "Patty, can you go tell whoever's still waiting to be seen that there will be about a forty-minute wait while I handle this emergency? Judy can reschedule them if they prefer not to wait. Then tell Vic that I need him to assist me, and you can run the anesthesia."

"Sure, Doc."

"I'll go to the waiting room," Baye said. She realized it was going to get crowded in this small room. "Will you be okay, Connie?"

"Yes, dear." She wiped a tear that had escaped her lashes. "I'll be fine as soon as he is. I don't know what I'd do without this little man."

Badger's short tail thumped against the examination table, and he licked her hand.

Baye followed Patty back to the waiting room and stood while she announced that everyone's appointments would be delayed.

"Oh, no," said one older lady, her arms around a trembling pit bull sitting on the bench next to her. "Is he hurt badly?"

"He'll be fine," Baye told them. "Unless Dr. Jayne finds some injury we can't see, he just needs his wound cleaned out and stitched."

They all nodded.

A middle-aged woman stood. "I've got to pick up the kids from soccer practice. Will Dr. Jayne be able to see me if I come back in about an hour?"

The vet tech looked to the receptionist who kept the schedule and received a firm nod. "Sure. We'll stay until everybody has been seen."

Baye took the woman's seat. It had been an exhausting day of crises. She called Teague to relay what the vet told her and Connie. When she hung up, the other three people waiting were staring at her.

"What happened? Did he get hit by a car?" a man holding a chihuahua asked.

"A bear came into my neighbor's pasture, where she has a few goats and sheep," Baye said. She loved being the center of attention and described the event in dramatic detail.

"He actually bit the bear on the butt?" asked a second man, who had a very obedient Doberman sitting at his feet. He shook his head. "I guess bravery comes in all sizes."

"Poor little thing," the woman with the pit bull said.

"I'm not surprised," the man with a chihuahua said. "I had a Jack Russell terrier once. He weighed twenty pounds, and I saw him latch onto a big rottweiler's back leg because he was chasing our cat. That rottie yelped like he'd been shot and ran back to his own house down the street."

They all laughed, and Baye marveled at how pets could become common ground for a group of people from all backgrounds, regardless of religious beliefs or politics. The waiting room went quiet when Connie appeared from the hallway with a groggy Badger, his head lolling against her shoulder.

"He's all patched up but still very sleepy." She choked out the words, a few tears escaping her bloodshot eyes.

Everyone, even the receptionist, applauded. Baye's storytelling had made the wait seem short, and now she wrapped an arm around Connie's shoulders.

"Well, let's get the hero home so he can sleep it off."

A chorus of "bye" followed them to the door.

❖

John was sitting in a camp chair on the back side of the kennel and cathouse buildings, a shotgun laid across his knees.

"Have you seen the bear?" Teague asked. She scanned the edge of the woods for movement.

"Nope. He's probably long gone," John said, never taking his gaze from the woods.

"Badger bit that bear on the butt," Tommy said.

John chuckled. "Did he now? He's a very brave dog."

"He's very, very brave. That bear was big!" Tommy stared at the shotgun in John's lap and began to sway back and forth, clearly stressed about something. "Are you going to hurt the bear if he comes here?"

"No, son. This only has salt shot in it. The salt will sting and scare it off, but not injure it." He turned to Teague. "How's your pup?"

"Baye called to say they were on their way home," Teague said. "He is still sleepy, but X-rays showed no hidden damage. He only needed stitches."

John nodded. "Tommy, why don't you go feed the kitties,

and I'll start feeding the dogs. When we're done, we'll lock everything up tight. I'm going to take Buster to the cottage with us. He'll hear that bear if he comes back."

"Good idea," Teague said. "I will help you feed."

CHAPTER THIRTEEN

Baye was alone on the sofa in the den, Cappie snuggled against her chest and Mac perched on her leg, grooming himself.

Teague kept her voice low. "How is Badger?"

"Doing better than Connie. He's technically your dog, but his heart belongs to her. She's very upset over his injury, but I think she's mostly scared that he could have been killed."

She sat on the sofa next to Baye and ran a finger over Cappie's head. He looked at her but didn't move into her lap or on her shoulder as she expected. Mac, however, pulled her arm down with his beak so he could step onto her forearm. "I believe you have stolen the heart of my little Captain."

"I love you," Mac said.

"I love you, too, Mac. Give me a kiss."

Mac bussed her lips with his beak, and then Baye reached over to turn Teague's chin her way for a real kiss, long and soft.

Teague's face heated, and a familiar tingle rolled through her belly. "Will you stay here tonight? I do not want you alone in your house in case the bear comes back."

"Is the bear the only reason you want me to stay?"

"No." Teague searched for the words to explain what she was feeling. "Today has been stressful. Being near you calms me." She took Baye's hand in hers. "At the same time, being near you excites me." She stared into Baye's hazel eyes, swirling with brilliant greens and rich browns. "It is a contradiction I do not fully understand."

Baye stood. "Let's put the kids to bed and see if we can explore the 'excites me' part."

Teague stood, her heart beating faster and her mind racing, and offered Baye her hand to also stand. Together, they returned Mac and Cappie to their cages in the sunroom. Then Baye took Teague's hand, and they walked to her bedroom.

Baye knew she had to take the lead because of Teague's uncertainty. When they reached the bedroom, she kissed her with all her emotion and reassurance, then stepped back and peeled off her T-shirt.

Teague licked her lips, her eyes fixed on Baye's sports bra.

"Will you help me?" Baye asked, lifting her arms over her head.

Teague hesitantly slipped her fingers under the chest band and lifted the bra over Baye's head. Baye stilled to let her look, then grasped her hands and placed them on her breasts. Teague closed her eyes, and her breath hitched. Baye held Teague's hands in place and stepped closer to kiss her long and deep until Teague responded, lifting and massaging Baye's breasts and tweaking her nipples.

Baye moaned into Teague's hot mouth. "That feels so good."

Teague stepped back and stripped off her T-shirt, then shed her bra. Her breasts were small, and a flush reddened her chest.

"Tell me if I do something that makes you uncomfortable," Baye said. "Can I touch your breasts?"

"I…I…yes."

Baye kissed her again, lightly caressing her nipples, then breaking off their kiss to take them in her mouth. Teague trembled when Baye scraped her teeth over her hard nipples, then sucked and nipped. "Let's get in the bed, baby." Baye cringed at her slip of an endearment. She was so afraid of going too fast and Teague backing off. Teague did back up, but only to strip off her jeans and underwear and pull the bedcovers down.

Baye was surprised for an instant, then quickly shed the rest of her clothes, too, and climbed into the bed. They both groaned when they came together naked, nipples touching nipples, and hips melding together. Teague flipped Baye onto her back and moved down to suck Baye's nipples, then lower to take her in her mouth. Baye was losing the battle to hold back her orgasm as Teague's relentless tongue bathed her in all the right places. Quick. It was too quick.

Her chest heaved. "Put your fingers inside me. Please, baby."

Teague's long fingers filled her, and she surrendered. "Teague. Oh, God. I'm coming." Her shoulders rose as her orgasm exploded and rolled through her belly. When her orgasm released its grip, she fell back onto the pillows, and Teague withdrew her fingers.

Before she could find her voice, Teague pushed her knees to her chest and moved to hover over her. She began to rub her sex against Baye's, the glide hot and smooth with the lubrication from them both. Her thrusts grew frantic, and she bore down harder.

"That's it, baby. Oh. I'm going to come again." Just as a second orgasm overcame Baye, Teague stiffened. Their cries rang out together, Teague riding her through the aftershocks until they both collapsed, sweaty and sated, to lie side by side.

"Wow." Baye's heart was still pounding. She was panting like she'd run a race. Their consummation had been quick and hard, but she vowed the next time would be slower. Oh, yes. There would be a next time. And a next and a next, if she had any say.

"Wow." Teague echoed her. "I…I."

Baye rolled onto her side and laid her hand between Teague's breasts. She could feel Teague's heart beating as fast as hers, in sync with hers. "What, Teague? You can tell me. Was it too much for you?"

Teague shook her head slowly. "I have lain with women before. Twice." Her chest rose and fell with a deep sigh. "But sex has never felt like this." She raised her eyes to meet Baye's and held her gaze for the longest few seconds yet. "This was more. A lot more."

Baye brushed her lips against Teague's and whispered, "For me, too. It's because of the feelings we have for each other that make it more."

"I want to hold you now, but my feelings are too big." Her eyes begged for understanding.

Baye lay back so that only their shoulders touched. "It's okay. It's been an adrenaline-filled day, and we just took a big step. We can take the smaller ones later." She felt the tension drain from Teague's muscles.

"Will you hold my hand…like before when I had a headache?"

Baye reached for her hand and entwined their fingers. "Anything you need, baby." The endearment slipped easily from her tongue now, and Teague didn't flinch. "Now sleep. Everyone is safe."

Chapter Fourteen

Teague woke to a light tapping on her bedroom door that led to the foyer. Baye was warm and soft spooned against her back, and she smiled to herself. The digital clock indicated it was seven in the morning. Damn, she never slept past five, but she didn't want to rise from the cocoon created by Baye and the plush comforter that covered them.

A second round of tapping was louder than the first.

"Teague, are you awake? Are you okay, honey?"

Teague had been sick the few times Connie had to wake her in the mornings. "I am okay. Just a minute." She gently disentangled herself from Baye's grasp and slipped on her robe before opening the door a few inches. "Sorry. I guess I overslept. Is Badger okay?"

"He's fine. Very sore, but he ate his breakfast and is napping after I gave him a pain pill," Connie said. "The rangers are here and want to talk to you about the bear."

She opened the door wider to peek through the vertical windows that flanked the front door. "Please ask them to give me a few minutes to get dressed."

Connie glanced past her and smiled. "I'm sorry, dear. I didn't know you had company."

Teague glanced over her shoulder and saw Baye still asleep, but now sprawled on top of Teague's pillow. Although nothing immodest was on display, the comforter had slipped down to her waist, and her bare back clearly revealed she was naked. Teague's face heated.

"I'll ask them to wait," Connie said, still smiling.

Teague closed the door quietly, then dressed in the jeans and T-shirt she'd shed the night before. She would shower and dress in clean clothes after talking to the ranger. She quickly washed her face and brushed her teeth, then glanced up at the mirror. Her hair was sticking out in a dozen directions. They had made love, slept a little, and made love again. She smiled at the memory of Baye pulling at her hair as Teague devoured her. A quick brushing mostly tamed it, and she tiptoed past her still-slumbering lover.

❖

"Hello. I am Teague Maxwell. I called you yesterday about the bear."

The man in a park ranger's uniform broke off his conversation with the others and held out his hand as he approached. "Hi. I'm Mike Barnes, one of the park rangers." He pointed to an attractive blond woman, then to the other man. "This is Dr. Ann Langston, a forestry department veterinarian, and Rick Seagrove, an experienced tracker."

She ignored the ranger's hand but nodded to each of them. She especially didn't like to touch strangers. "Thank you for coming."

"We would like to park our truck here," Ranger Barnes said. "Tom, the ranger that took your call, said he told you the bear's collar has malfunctioned and is no longer transmitting, so we're going to have to track and dart him. Do you have time to show us where the bear came over your fence?"

"Yes. We confined our animals to the barn last night, so I need to let them out into the pasture. Just follow me." Snow, who Connie always fed at the house with Badger, joined them.

The three shouldered light backpacks and walked with her to the barn, where she released Lucky and Asset first, then the sheep and goats, and finally the chickens. She gave the rabbits a few extra treats since they hadn't gotten to go out the night before. Even though they were very large rabbits, they stayed in the barn during the daytime because several eagles nested nearby and might decide to snack on them. While the others immediately began grazing or scratching among the grass for insects and worms, the goats and Asset decided to escort the ranger's group, just in case those backpacks contained treats.

"We're pretty sure your bear was a two-year-old male recently tagged about ten miles from here as soon as he parted from his mother. I'm sure he was looking for food and his own territory to hunt. He won't be searching for a mate for a year or two."

The veterinarian, Dr. Langston, stepped closer and smiled. "I bet our bear was very surprised after he climbed over your fence. You've got quite a squad of defenders."

"He was after the fainting goats, which are easy prey." She pointed to Asset, then Lucky. "Those two herded the sheep into that corner over there and stood guard." She scratched behind Snow's ear. "My farm hand, Tommy, is a large man. He grabbed a pitchfork, and then he and Snow confronted the bear. I was alerted when my parrot, who had been with Tommy, flew up to the house screaming. Baye and I ran to the barn and stood next to Tommy, shouting and waving our arms. The real hero is our twenty-pound terrier that bit the bear in the butt and sent him running."

Dr. Langston put her hand on Teague's shoulder and laughed loudly. "A terrier? Where is he?"

Teague turned to discreetly move out of Dr. Langston's reach and pointed to the house. "He was clawed when the bear swiped at him to make him let go, so Connie has him under house arrest until he is sufficiently healed. The wound is not too serious. He only needed some stitches to patch him up."

The two men were walking back and forth, examining the tracks left in the ground still soft from recent rain.

"Poor thing. He's a brave little dog to go after a bear." Dr. Langston dug into her backpack for a business card and scribbled something on the back, then handed it to Teague. "You can call me if he has any complications. Day or night. I'd be happy to come check him out."

Teague stuffed the card into her pocket without reading it. "Thank you, but his vet says he will be fine."

The two men approached. "Looks like he headed straight into the woods," Rick, the tracker, said. "He might still be hanging around and double back to try some other farms along this border. I'd keep putting your animals up at night until we catch this fellow."

"You will let me know when you do?" Teague asked.

"Give me your phone, and I'll put my number in your contacts," Dr. Langston said.

Teague hesitated. She couldn't explain why, but it felt wrong to give a woman her number. "I sometimes do not answer my phone or check my voice mail for days when I am working. I will give you my house manager's number. Or my neighbor's number. Tommy works for both of us. He takes care of my animals in addition to the cats and dogs at Baye's rescue center next door."

"Ah. Baye is your neighbor?"

Teague cocked her head to consider this question. "Yes. She is also my girlfriend." She liked how "girlfriend" rolled so easily off her tongue.

Dr. Langston shrugged and handed Teague a small notepad. "It was worth a try. If you will write Connie's number down for me, I'll give her a call when we find the bear."

❖

Teague stopped in the doorway of her bedroom and frowned. The shower was running even though the bathroom door was open, and Baye was missing from the bed. She had wanted to wake Baye up while she was still naked. Then the shower stopped while she was making the bed. She always kept neat rooms, so the cleaning agency only had to dust, vacuum, and clean the bathroom in her downstairs suite.

"Hey, you. Where'd you go?" Baye stood in the bathroom doorway, wrapped in a thick towel that barely covered her breasts and touched her thighs. "I missed you when I woke up."

"The ranger and the people who are going to track the bear showed up early and wanted to talk to me about yesterday." Teague stripped as she talked. "The woman veterinarian with them said we should keep the animals in the barn at night until she calls to say they caught the bear." She pulled the business card from her pocket and handed it to Baye before tossing her jeans in the hamper.

"Did she now?" Baye turned the card over. "Is this her personal number?"

"I suppose. I did not look at it. I told her I sometimes do not answer my phone or check my voice mail for days when I am working, so she should call Connie or you. She wrote down Connie's number but did not take yours."

"Why not?"

"I told her you were my girlfriend."

Baye laughed. "She was hitting on you."

"Dr. Langston did put her hand on my shoulder." Teague frowned. "I do not like people touching me."

"Really?" Baye dropped her towel and pressed her breasts against Teague's now-naked form. "You don't like this?" She ran her hand over Teague's butt.

Teague smiled and closed her eyes. "I do like your touch, but we do not have time for sex. Connie is cooking breakfast for us, and I need to shower."

Baye stepped away but grabbed Teague's hand. "I'll wash your back."

❖

"Pretty, kiss Pretty," Mac called from his perch, ruffling his feathers, bobbing his head, and swaying back and forth. Cappie scampered in from the sunroom and held his arms out for Baye to pick him up. Then she walked over to Mac to let him buss her lips with his beak.

"How quickly they abandon you for a pretty face," Teague said.

"Glad you two could finally join us." Connie grinned as she took two plates holding huge omelets from the oven and placed them on the kitchen island.

Teague shrugged and settled in a bar chair on the other side of the island. "Baye wanted to have sex in the shower."

Baye whirled around, heat infusing her face. "Teague!"

Connie burst out in a hearty laugh and crossed the room to give Baye a one-armed hug. "It's all right, sweetie. We're all family here. She has a hard time knowing what should stay private. Juice or coffee?"

"She is my girlfriend." Teague's tone was matter-of-fact.

A different kind of warmth filled Baye's chest every time Teague said that. She kissed Teague's cheek as she settled into the chair next to her. "Yes, and you are mine." She smiled at Connie. "Can I have both?"

"Yes, you can," Connie said as she placed a large bowl of fruit cubes between them. "Y'all go ahead. I ate hours ago when I got up to feed the dogs and give Badger his medication."

"Bless his heart. He's such a brave little guy," Baye said. Her heart had been in her throat when he bit the bear. She was sure the bear would turn and grab him up in his jaws.

Connie sniffed, her eyes tearing a bit. "Yes, he is. In fact, I better go check on him to see if he needs to go out."

"Remember, the vet said to put him on a leash outside," Baye said. "He needs to walk to keep from getting stiff, but he shouldn't run until the stitches heal a little."

"I remember," Connie said, waving over her shoulder.

Baye took a large bite of her omelet. "Oh my God. This is so good."

"Yes," Teague said. "She has cooked for my family since I was a child." She stopped eating and stared at her plate. "Sometimes when I was little, I wished she had adopted me instead of my parents. They were good to me, but when they found out that I was different from other children, I think my mother regretted having me."

"Oh, honey. My parents were great, too, but I just wore them out."

"Are they still alive?"

"Yes. But I only talk to them a few times a year." She couldn't tell Teague that they'd taken out a second mortgage on their house to bail her out of financial trouble about seven years ago and she hadn't paid back any of it. They both had to postpone retirement to make the payments. She'd distanced herself from them since because of the shame she felt. She wanted to be better. To do better. Teague had learned to manage her disability, so maybe she could, too.

They finished eating, and Teague cleaned up after them while Connie was walking Badger.

"So, what's on your agenda today?" Baye asked. "Should I go home so you can work?"

"I would like to see what progress you have made finding suitable homes for my animals."

Shit. "Um, sure. We can take our coffee out to the terrace, and I'll give you a summary of my progress. I don't have my notes here, so I can't really give you details." She'd done little more than browse the web and solicit interested people through social media. She received hundreds of instant messages from all over the country but hadn't read many of them. She planned to make a spreadsheet of the offers for Teague to review, but she'd spent the past week getting high and sulking about Teague's behavior when she was working.

"Then we will go to your house."

"NO. I mean, I haven't had a chance to clean it up." *Think fast, think fast.* "It's a mess because I was depressed after you threw me out of the cottage because you were working. It was like you had forgotten who I was. I was devastated."

"I am very sorry, but your house should be clean now."

"What? Do you employ elves that go around and clean other people's houses?"

"Not elves. I asked Connie to send our cleaning agency to your house yesterday afternoon as an apology for my behavior. I forgot to tell you because the bear distracted us."

"Really?"

"I always tell the truth."

Baye was delighted. "Yes, you do." She laughed and kissed Teague's cheek. "Like you telling Connie we were late to breakfast because we were having shower sex."

"It is the truth."

Baye had to laugh again at the puzzlement on Teague's face. If she ever suspected her of cheating, all she would have to do was ask. Teague would surely answer truthfully. She kissed her again, this time on the lips. "Yes, it is. Let's go see what my house looks like clean."

❖

"Wow. I can't believe this is the same house my grandmother lived in." Baye was amazed by the job Teague's agency had done. Not only had they cleaned up Baye's mess, but they had also removed years of dirt wedged in cracks, covering baseboards, collecting on ceiling fans, darkening tile grout, and clinging to walls. "It's spotless. Even the air in here smells clean."

"The report Connie received said the filters to the heating and cooling system were black with dirt and mold, so they also cleaned your ductwork."

"Uh, what's ductwork?"

Teague's eyebrows rose in an incredulous expression. "Do you even know where your fuse box is?"

"What?" She made an impatient noise. "Just because I'm a lesbian doesn't mean I'm handy with tools and such. I do know that every house has an electrical box. I'm just not sure where mine is."

"Noted." Teague's smile was wry.

Baye spotted Tommy and John out by the dog pens. Maybe she could distract Teague from checking her progress on rehoming her pets. "Hey, we should update John and Tommy on the bear situation. You know, find out if they've seen any sign of the bear prowling around the kennels."

Teague looked through the window, too, and nodded. "We should let John know about the three people tracking the bear. I would not want him to shoot salt at them if he sees them in the woods behind the kennels."

Shoot salt? She had no idea what Teague was talking about, but she'd go with it. "Right. I was thinking the same thing."

Tommy and John were swapping out dogs to give all of them time in the play yards. The pool had been a big hit, so there was now one in each yard.

Baye was surprised to see Buster, the hugely muscular pit bull, playing in the yard that held a dozen small dogs. "John, is it wise to let him in with the little dogs? He could snatch one of those chihuahuas up and kill it with one shake of his head."

"Oh, no!" Tommy said. "Buster won't hurt any of them. He likes them."

John chuckled. "We actually have a lot fewer dustups with him in there babysitting."

As if on cue, a chihuahua guarding a small ball jumped another that walked too close. Buster was there in an instant, sticking his big head between the two. This move stopped the assault, but the angry dog went after his perceived thief a second time. Buster, tail wagging, gently wrapped his jaw around the tiny dog's shoulders, picked him up like a puppy, and walked across the yard to plop him down in a far corner.

"She's being a bad dog, and Buster has put her in time-out," Tommy explained. "Now, he'll play with her until she isn't mad anymore."

Baye watched in amazement as the big dog licked the tiny dog, then lay down and rolled onto his back, inviting the chihuahua to climb on him and playfully nip at him. "That is so sweet."

"You should keep Buster to help manage the other animals and guard the kennels," Teague said.

"Could we? I've never had a dog of my own." Tommy looked hopefully at Baye. "He could sleep with me at night and listen for bears and help with the other dogs. He's really good."

Baye, of course, melted and instantly wanted to grant Tommy's request. Teague was more practical.

"You would have to bathe him every week, maybe more often if he gets muddy or rolls in something stinky."

"He loves a bath," Tommy said, his eyes glowing.

"You will be responsible for feeding him, keeping his nails trimmed, and making sure he goes outside to potty," Teague said.

The big man grinned. "I already do that, and he never goes potty inside."

"Also, I do not want you to bring him up to my barn until I can meet you there and make sure he is going to be okay around Mac, Cappie, the rabbits, and the chickens. I will need to introduce him to Lucky and Asset, too, so they will not think he will hurt the sheep or goats."

Tommy nodded. "Yes, ma'am. Can we do that soon?"

"How about tomorrow? Leave him here with John when you come over to feed and put everyone in the barn tonight."

"Okay." Tommy began to rock back and forth with excitement.

Baye added one last condition. "You have to ask John if it's okay for you to have a dog. You live in his house."

"John, please, can Buster be my dog and live with us?"

John scratched at his beard stubble as though thinking it over. "You'll have to wash your sheets and blanket every week if he sleeps on your bed, and you'll have to vacuum the rugs and clean the floors every other week. Dogs shed their hair and track in dirt a lot. I can mark it on your chore calendar for you."

Tommy nodded vigorously.

"Then I guess Buster can live with us."

Tommy nearly knocked John over with a bear hug. "Thank you, thank you." Then he rushed to Baye and hugged her. When he looked at Teague, Baye thought she was going to run from his exuberance. "Miss Baye said you don't like to be hugged unless it's her doing it. So, can she hug you for me?"

Baye laughed at the relief on Teague's face as she smiled and nodded. "I can do that," she said, then gave her a long, firm hug. "You have to come up to the house after you put the dogs back in their kennels and sign Buster's adoption papers so he will really be yours." *Ah. Another delay. Maybe Teague will forget reviewing her rehoming project today.*

Tommy hesitated. "Do I need money to adopt Buster?"

Baye smiled at him. He really was a kid in a man's body. "Nope. You get the employee discount, which means Buster is free."

❖

"So, I posted on multiple social media platforms to solicit applications from suitable pet lovers, and I got hundreds of responses. I'm printing the emails and copying the instant messages so I can enter them in a spreadsheet to filter out the best prospects." She sent several of the emails to the printer to demonstrate. "I'll send emails to the best ones to get more detailed or missing information, so we can narrow them down even further. I'll weed out, of course, any that reply from outside the United States." Baye paused and looked up from the email account she'd set up just to collect responses. "Should I narrow it down to the East Coast or just to the Southeast?"

"No," Teague said. "Anywhere in this country…and maybe Canada." She went to the printer and scanned a couple of the emails.

"I've been working on setting up separate spreadsheets for Asset, Lucky, Mac, Cappie, Snow, Leo, the chickens, the rabbits, the goats, and the sheep. I have so many emails, it will take a while to input the information into the spreadsheets."

Teague looked puzzled. "I am paying you five thousand a month. You can hire someone to help you with the mundane tasks like inputting information."

Baye was surprised. "Oh. I hadn't thought of that."

"You could post some flyers around the university campus to find a college student who needs a summer job. You should post flyers in the building where they teach statistics. Those students should be accomplished at spreadsheets."

"That's a great idea." Baye kissed Teague on the cheek. "That's why you're a genius." She debated, then decided to voice what had nagged at her from the beginning. "Can I ask a question?"

"Of course." Teague didn't look up from studying the categories on the spreadsheet.

"Why don't you just set up a trust for someone to live in your house and care for the animals after you, uh…are gone? They could live out their lives in the home they've come to know."

Teague sat back. "My estate has been passed down through three generations of Maxwells by a transfer-on-death deed stipulating that upon the owner's death, the estate is automatically transferred to the nearest blood relative in the Maxwell family. I have no heir, so the estate will automatically go to my male cousin, who is allergic to both fur and feathers."

"I see. What if your animals simply came to live with me? You know I love all of them."

"I do not see that as a viable solution because of your proximity to their current home. You would be constantly retrieving them from the estate because they would seek to go to their old home at every opportunity." She paused. "And, given your, um, lax housekeeping, this house would not be a safe environment for Max or Cappie."

Baye stiffened. "I just kind of let things go when I get depressed. Then when things pile up, I'm too overwhelmed to know where to start cleaning up. I can do better."

"And I can start hugging every person I see." Teague's tone, her fleeting gaze were kind. "We both have to face the reality of our struggles."

Baye didn't like it, but Teague was right. Even if she could afford to hire a housekeeper, they wouldn't be with her twenty-four hours a day, every day of the year. Teague's obsession with neatness and routine created the ideal environment for the inquisitive parrot and monkey. Even when Teague was in manic work mode, she kept them with her in the cottage to tend to their basic needs.

"I thought you would be farther along on the project," Teague said. "We're going into the second month."

"Well…"

Teague's phone rang, and she glanced at the display. "It is the hospital." She accepted the call. "Hello…yes, this is Teague Maxwell…I can be there in ten minutes." She nodded as if the person on the other end could see her. "Thank you." She ended the call. "I have an ultrasound of my heart scheduled for next week, but they have had a cancellation and want me to come now."

Baye stood when Teague did. "Do you want me to go with you?"

"No. It will not take long, and there is no sedation involved.

Results will not be available until tomorrow." She started for the door, but Baye stopped her for a long kiss.

"Will you call me when you get home?"

"Yes."

Chapter Fifteen

Take off your shirt and bra and put on this gown so that it opens in the front," the ultrasound technician said before drawing a curtain around the space that contained a chair and a large hamper for discarded gowns. "Just come on out when you're ready."

The gown didn't make sense to Teague. The minute she lay down on the bed, the technician would open it and expose her breasts anyway. Why couldn't she just shuck off her shirt and bra and lie down? She and the technician were the only ones in the room. She sighed and did as instructed anyway. She was grateful the gel the technician spread on her chest was warm, but the slide of the ultrasound wand against her skin made her grind her teeth and clinch the sides of the table. She closed her eyes and imagined Baye was holding the ultrasound wand, not some women she met five minutes ago.

"Is your doctor looking for something specific?" the technician asked.

"Yes. We are looking for any indication of an aneurysm."

"Gotcha. I didn't have the full order handy since we bumped up your appointment. Thanks, by the way, for coming in so quickly."

"You are welcome." Teague waited impatiently. Just when she thought she was about to jump off the table and flee, the technician began to wipe her chest with a towel.

"All done."

"What did you see?"

"Oh, I don't read the results. A doctor will do that. Someone should call you tomorrow with them."

"You do a lot of these tests?"

"Yep. I've been in this lab for the past fifteen years."

"So, you should know if you see an irregularity. What did you see?"

"I suppose it wouldn't hurt to tell you. You appear to have a perfectly healthy heart. That is not a doctor's opinion, though, so you should wait for him to call you after he's read the ultrasound."

"Thank you."

❖

"We're taking the first step in collider technology that will make the huge rocket boosters obsolete. Nuclear fusion and the theoretical quark fusion are useless unless we figure out how to construct a collider small enough to be mobile. Think flux-capacitor and warp-drive engineering. It's all theory right now, but we need help working on the mathematics to lay the groundwork," Dr. Robert Turner said.

The idea was intriguing, even enticing. It was the exact problem Teague had privately been exploring for years in her spare time. "I appreciate your faith in me, but this is not something I can work out in a few months, or even a year, and give you definitive results," she said.

He laughed. "You are brilliant, but I wasn't proposing that. We want to hire you to lead a team of scientists on this project long-term."

"I work alone, Dr. Turner. You know that. And I will not relocate."

"I'm aware of your personal challenges, Dr. Maxwell. I'm asking you to pinpoint the hurdles to this technology, then recommend teams of scientists to focus on specific problems. You would be the puzzle master, fitting together the pieces they produce. You would be expected to meet periodically—maybe a few times a year—with the teams that you assign to individual projects."

"Why do you want me to lead this study?"

"To be frank, Dr. Maxwell, we both know your brain is wired a bit differently. While you might see that as challenging, NASA sees it as an asset. We need someone who can look at the map and see a different, unexpected route to the solution. Does that make sense?"

"Yes." She was excited by the challenge, but something she couldn't yet define made her hesitate. She'd worked on several projects for Dr. Turner and respected his expertise. They were more than acquaintances but not really friends. She didn't have friends. "I will consider your offer, Dr. Turner, and give you an answer within the week. Will that be sufficient?"

"Yes. Thank you. I hope you will accept, but I can wait. You have my number, so give me a call when you decide."

"I will. Good-bye."

❖

"Hey, you. How'd your test go?"

"I will not get official results from the doctor until tomorrow, but I bullied the technician into giving me her opinion, compared to the many other ultrasounds she has performed." As promised, she had called Baye after she arrived back home and invited her over for dinner.

"I'm sure you did," Bay said, smiling. "And she said—"

"She said my heart looked very healthy as far as she could tell."

"Good." She patted Teague's chest. "I already knew a good, strong heart beats in there."

"I am still waiting for the genetic-testing results, which could indicate if I have an increased chance of developing an aortic aneurysm."

"They're more common in men. I looked it up," Baye said.

"Brain aneurysms are more prevalent among women, and I have not had my MRI yet. My father died of a heart aneurysm, and his mother of the Maxwell bloodline died of a brain aneurysm," she said. "My great-great-grandfather and my great-great-great-grandmother are believed to have died of a brain aneurysm. There were no autopsies, but both are reported to have complained of a severe headache immediately prior to collapsing."

"I can see why you would be worried, but have you considered that your brain might be different from others in your family? Have any of your relatives been on the autism spectrum before you?"

"No, but the first diagnosis of autism was not recognized until 1943. Like a lot of mental illness, people before that were considered mentally deficient, and most were committed to institutions. Some families institutionalized a child, then pretended they were never born."

"Ha. Not here in the South. We're proud of our eccentric family members." The conversation was growing too serious, so Baye felt she should try to lighten the mood. "We even seat them on the front porch to wave to the neighbors."

"That is odd behavior," Teague said, cocking her head as if trying to understand.

Baye sighed. Humor was mostly wasted on Teague.

"Did you work on the spreadsheets this afternoon?" Teague asked.

"No. I made a flyer to advertise for some part-time help and posted some copies at the university."

"That is good. It is too soon to expect a response."

"Actually, when I put one on the message board at the student union, a student saw it and chased me down to apply for the job. So, we went back into the building and talked over coffee. She has a financial-aid grant that pays for her books and tuition, but she needs a part-time job to pay for food and her room in the dorm. I liked her, so I hired her. She starts tomorrow afternoon."

"Very good." Teague paused. "I was offered a new contract today."

"To solve another problem for NASA?" The unpleasant, work-mode Teague was still fresh in her mind. "Are you going to disappear for days into your cottage again?"

"Maybe a few days, but not like last time."

"Good. I didn't like the argument we had then. And I'll miss you, but I understand you have to work."

"I did not like our argument either, so I have not agreed to do it. I do enjoy working, but I do not need to. I have more money than I can spend. However, I do not want to anger you or accept a project I will not live long enough to complete."

Baye took a deep breath. "First of all, if you stop doing the work you love, you will grow to resent me. So, don't turn it down because of me…because of us. Second, you never answered my question." She desperately wanted Teague to stop this I'm-going-to-die notion.

"I have considered that I might be exempt from the aneurysm curse since my brain is not very similar to those in my bloodline." Although Teague sometimes had trouble staying on subject in a conversation, she had no problem picking up a dropped thread. Her memory was near eidetic. "But I will not rely on that. I prefer science to chance. I must be prepared for any outcome."

Baye leaned close and brushed her lips against Teague's. "I don't want to think about possibly losing you. I just found you."

Puzzlement filled Teague's features. "I have been right here, living next door to you."

Baye laughed and pulled Teague into a tight hug. "Yes, you have."

"What is her name?" Teague asked.

"Who?"

"The student."

"Oh. Their name is TJ."

"You hired more than one?"

"No, honey. TJ is nonbinary and uses the pronouns they and them."

"Okay. I am familiar with using ambiguous pronouns. I have considered doing the same. Teague was considered a female name in the Southern states during the 1800s, but people seem to identify it as a male-oriented name now. I am often called sir."

"Good to know."

"Baye?"

"Yes?" She loosened her hug but gave in to the urge to trail kisses along Teague's neck.

Teague spoke softly. "I do not want to die. I just found you."

"I'm right here, living next door."

CHAPTER SIXTEEN

Baye was bored and restless because Teague was at NASA for four days. She was due back tomorrow, and Baye couldn't wait. She missed her stilted speech, those beautiful dark eyes that struggled to meet hers, and the fleeting seconds when they did. She missed Teague's puzzlement over things that weren't practical or logical, and her inability to lie or scheme. And she missed that tall, strong body—firm, long muscles and soft, soft skin—covering hers. Often halting and clumsy in her speech and movements, she was neither as a lover. Teague the lover was like someone with a severe stutter who showed no sign of the impediment when they sang.

She and Teague had worked together to set up the adoption spreadsheets before she left, and TJ was diligently working to fill them in from the emails and instant messages. Baye was still receiving up to thirty a day. She got hundreds of inquiries about Mac, Cappie, or Flower, but most had little or no experience with exotic animals. Leo's placement was going to be easy. Apparently, a lot of cat lovers adored the Maine coon breed. Only a few, however, were offering to take in Asset, Lucky, Snow, the goats, the sheep, or the rabbits with the stipulations Teague had set down. The goats, sheep, and rabbits could not be killed for meat or resold. Lucky and Snow needed to work to be happy, and Asset was not to be used for labor unless it was guard duty. He also needed interaction with people.

Baye fidgeted. She had wanted to shop for a new laptop for TJ to use, but Libby insisted the expense was unnecessary and shared the spreadsheets in the Google cloud so TJ could access them from her school laptop. Bummer. Baye liked to shop. She stared at the ceiling. Libby and her budget took the fun out of everything.

Libby had quit her waitressing job and moved back into the farmhouse after Connie had sent her cleaning agency to tackle the trash dump Baye had created, then scheduled them to return one day a week. Because they did the heavy cleaning—dusting, mopping, and cleaning the bathrooms—Libby didn't complain about picking up after Baye in the common rooms. She didn't ask who was paying for the crew. At least it wasn't on Heavy Petting's expense sheet.

Libby also caught up with the review of applications for the rescue's adoptable animals, then turned that job back over to Baye so she could concentrate on filing quarterly taxes, tracking payroll and other expenses, and trolling for grants or other sources of income for their nonprofit. Libby was constantly reminding Baye that Heavy Petting needed to be able to operate in the near future without Teague's five thousand every month. They wouldn't have that extra money forever, she said. Baye would give it up tomorrow if it meant Teague was healthy and didn't die young.

Damn it. She was bored and restless. Sprawled on the sofa, she peeked over the back of it at TJ, who sat at the dining room table working on the spreadsheets.

She'd primarily hired TJ because they seemed smart and had almost begged for the job. She also identified nonbinary TJ as one of the misunderstood and often alienated people, like her and Teague. TJ wasn't just androgynous. Their ears were full of piercings, and their lobes stretched around circular gauges Baye could almost put her thumb through. They also had piercings in their lip, nose, and an eyebrow. Both arms were covered in full-sleeve tattoos they said they'd paid for by working at the parlor where they were done. Baye had been impressed by TJ's knowledge of spreadsheets and their desperation for the job. If she was honest, though, she thought TJ would also be fun. She was so wrong.

Baye lay down so she was hidden by the back of the sofa and opened her pack of marijuana joints. The substance was legal in this state, and a few tokes would help calm her agitation. She flicked her lighter a few times and peeked over the sofa again.

"Libby said you aren't allowed to smoke that in the house." TJ didn't look up from their laptop.

"Come on. Let's go out on the porch, have a smoke, and then play with kittens." That was Baye's favorite self-prescribed therapy.

"Aren't you supposed to be answering those adoption applications?" TJ pointed to a stack of paper next to Baye's laptop at the other end of the table. "Libby printed them out for you."

"Hey! I'm your boss, and I say we go play with kittens."

"Libby says she's the boss of both of us."

"She thinks she is." Baye huffed. "You're a first-class imposter. How could I be so wrong about you?"

"Don't judge a book by its cover, or a person by their piercings," TJ said, head down and still typing. "I have homework to do later. If I smoke that stuff or inhale it secondhand from you, I'll never get it done."

Baye stood and hung her head, wallowing in dejection. "I miss my girlfriend."

TJ finally looked up and grinned. "You're pathetic. Get out of here. Go smoke and play with kittens. I'm way ahead of my daily goal. I can go through the applications for you."

Baye immediately brightened and trotted to the door. "Thank you. I owe you."

"Yeah, yeah. It's worth it to get you out of my hair," they said, laughing.

❖

Teague had barely exited her Jeep when Baye burst from her house, leapt down the steps, and jumped into her arms with such force she was slammed back against the vehicle.

"I missed you," Baye said, peppering her face with kisses, then taking her mouth in one long kiss.

She was startled at first but relaxed as Baye's arms and legs held her in a firm hug. Her body responded, leaving her brain stumbling to catch up. She'd never met anyone who could evoke such visceral responses from her. "I missed you, too. Very much." She locked her arms under Baye's buttocks and carried her into Baye's house and onto the sofa. "I need you. I need you now."

"Yes."

Baye's breath on her face, her lips on her neck—it was like finding that thread of an equation that pointed to a solution. Her need to feel her skin on Baye's consumed her like the drive to solve a problem. She stripped off her shirt and sports bra, then pulled Baye's T-shirt over her head and fumbled with her bra. Teague sucked in a breath and shivered when Baye unbuttoned and unzipped both of their jeans. Finally freeing the damned tiny hooks, she flung Baye's bra across the room, pressed their breasts together, and took her in a deep kiss. She slid her hand down Baye's soft belly and into her wet warmth at the same time Baye's fingers slid over her clit, causing Teague to break off their kiss and suck in a quick breath. Though with only a glance, she saw the heat, the passion in Baye's eyes as they stroked each other in perfect sync. Were the moans hers or Baye's? It didn't matter. Her head buzzed with the swell of discovery and approaching resolution. She might as well have been working on the elusive collider predicted to revolutionize energy. This woman with beautiful curls and hazel eyes had hurtled into her life, and their collision created a fusion she had no words to describe.

They both cried out as they climaxed almost simultaneously, then collapsed together on the narrow sofa. After a long moment of hard panting and hearts pounding, Baye shook with a lilting laugh.

"I think it's safe to say we missed each other." She pointed to Teague's eyes, then her own to direct Teague's gaze to hers, as she'd seen Connie do. "I love you," she said softly.

It was difficult, but Teague latched onto the swirls of green and gold in Baye's eyes. "I love you," she said.

They froze at the sound of a discreet cough in the dining room.

"Oh, shit." Baye had forgotten TJ was working inside. She grabbed her T-shirt that was draped haphazardly over the back of the sofa and pushed Teague up a bit. "Put this on," she whispered, awkwardly tugging one of Teague's arms through it, then pulling it over her head like she were dressing a child. Teague struggled onto her knees to push her other arm into the shirt without rising above the back of the sofa and exposing herself to TJ. Baye glanced around the room, then pointed to Teague's shirt on the floor just beyond her reach, still whispering. "Now get your shirt for me."

Without looking in the direction of the dining room, Teague refastened her jeans and crawled over to grab the shirt. "Who is that?" she asked Baye.

God almighty, this was going to be awkward. Baye slipped into Teague's shirt. "Stand up."

They stood together and turned to face TJ, who peeked over the screen of their laptop, their face a brilliant red. "I'm minding my own business, putting this stuff in the spreadsheets."

Baye chuckled. "Sorry about that. Like I said yesterday, I missed my girlfriend." She reached for Teague's hand. "This is Teague Maxwell. Teague, this is TJ, whose pronouns are 'they' and 'them.'" Teague frowned, and Baye held her breath, remembering their only real argument had started with what Teague perceived as a misuse of the English language. Would she refuse to use TJ's pronouns? She hurried to move past this possibility, hoping to distract Teague. "TJ is the student I told you about. They've done a really good job helping me organize all those emails into spreadsheets."

Teague turned her head as if considering something. "Do you belong to the Church of Body Modification? Or do you pierce your body for medical reasons?"

TJ glanced at Baye, then stood and rounded the table to face them. "Medical reasons?"

"Yes. I read once that many acupressure points in the ears and face can relieve pain if pierced. Also, some ancient cultures believed piercings could provide immunity from certain diseases. And, more recently, researchers are studying whether piercings or a pressure clamp on a certain part of the ear or face might help control obsessive-compulsive disorders and curb addictions."

"That's very interesting," TJ said. They shrugged. "I just did it because it's cool. You know…an expression of who I am. I've never heard of the Church of Body Modification, but maybe I'll look it up."

Teague nodded. "You can never gather too much knowledge. What are you studying at the university?"

"Finance and economics."

"Really?" Baye had never thought to ask TJ about their field of study. "What made you choose those fields?"

"I want to help marginalized people—women, minorities, LGBTQIA people, refugees, and homeless. Money is power. Most of these groups are held down by others that own the wealth in this world. Wealth is used to control the workforce, governments, education, and, in many cases, religion. The oppressed will never rise until we learn to tap into wealth and shift the power to make real change in the world."

Wow. Baye had never realized TJ ran so deep. She silently admonished herself for never thinking of TJ as anything more than a college student who was likely sabotaging their chances for a good job after graduation because of their nontraditional piercings and tattoos.

"You are correct," Teague said. "Without my family's wealth and connections to protect and nurture me, I might have been deprived of opportunities that have led to many of my patents and financial success. I would be interested in speaking with you at another time about your aspirations." She straightened Baye's T-shirt, which was a bit too big for her slender frame. "Presently, I am very tired from traveling, and I am afraid you have caught me literally with my pants down."

Baye stared at her, stunned for a moment. "Oh my God. Did you just make a joke? You did."

"I am capable of expressing humor," Teague deadpanned.

Baye wrapped Teague in a tight hug, trapping her arms against her body. "Yes, you are."

TJ stood and closed their laptop. "I'd like that. Baye says you're some kind of genius or something."

"I do have a very high IQ," Teague said. She was always truthful and matter-of-fact about it.

"Well, maybe I should go and leave you two alone."

"You do not have to leave. I am eager to see my animals, so I came to take Baye to my house for tonight."

"I was hoping you would want me to stay at your house," Baye said. "I've already packed an overnight bag." She retrieved the small suitcase at the bottom of the staircase.

TJ put their laptop down. "Maybe I'll stay here tonight?" They shot Baye a questioning look. "Libby said she was going to bring a pizza back."

"Absolutely," Baye said. In fact, she had been meaning to ask about TJ's living arrangements and offer them the third bedroom upstairs. They got along well with Libby and didn't seem to like the roommate they'd been assigned in the dorm. "You're more than welcome." She tugged Teague toward the door. "Let's go, Romeo. Connie and the kids will be ecstatic to see you're home."

Chapter Seventeen

"I don't have to tell you that this is a very unusual situation," Dr. Sylvia Hanson said. "I've worked with many clients diagnosed with ADHD, and several with varying degrees of autism spectrum disorder, or ASD, but never a couple who wanted to be treated together."

Teague nodded. She was aware they would be a notable case study. But she'd been a patient of Dr. Hansen's since she was a child and trusted her. "Some aspects of the two disorders manifest in totally opposite symptoms, but many of the suggested coping mechanisms are the same," she said.

"That's true," Dr. Hansen said. "Both of your disabilities—and they are classified as such under the American Disabilities Act—have been shown to benefit from adherence to a regular schedule and exercise. But there also are some radical differences in your symptoms. While Teague tends to hyper-focus on certain things, Baye finds it difficult to stay focused."

Baye had been reticent about therapy, and Teague worried she might leave the session if the doctor spent too much time talking about why this relationship might not work.

"We're hoping that our love and strong desire to please each other will help us find some middle ground," Baye said.

"That's the goal. Your desire not to let the other person down can be a very strong motivator. And support is vital."

When Baye reached for Teague's hand and held it firmly, Teague realized she'd been touching her thumb to each fingertip in a repetitive motion to calm her nerves. Was Baye holding her hand to reassure her or because the action was bothering her? No matter the reason, she gave Baye's fingers an affirming squeeze. They could do this.

Dr. Hanson gestured to their hands. "Just the fact that Teague tolerates you holding her hand is evidence your relationship has overcome her aversion to being touched." She held up a finger. "But you need to be aware of some real pitfalls in this venture. Baye's ADHD means she can tend to overreact emotionally, while Teague's ASD makes it difficult to express her emotions or recognize someone else's emotional crisis. Also, Teague can be overly sensitive to sound, smells, and general chaotic situations. People with ADHD tend to be grandiose—loud and chaotic—in their enthusiasm or when expressing displeasure, which could overwhelm someone with ASD and trigger a meltdown."

"We've both witnessed each other's meltdowns, and my need to comfort her pulled me right out of mine," Baye said.

"We have also survived a meltdown at each other," Teague added. "Knowing that our disabilities aggravated our disagreement made it possible for us to talk it out after a cool-down period."

"That's good, very good. But be aware that if you begin residing together, many more of these instances will come up, even over tiny differences. For example, Baye brushes her teeth but doesn't replace the cap on the toothpaste or rinse the sink after spitting her toothpaste into it," she said to Teague. "This bothers you, so you replace the cap on the toothpaste, then rinse the sink for her. Baye has wakened that morning feeling agitated for no explicable reason—because this happens sometimes for people with ADHD—and perceives your action as constant correction. She overreacts with explosive anger, yelling and using foul language. You may curl up in a ball to try to shut out her display or try to calm yourself with a repetitive motion, which agitates her even more."

Baye's face darkened. "You make it sound like I'm the reason you think this won't work."

"Not at all. Let's try a different scenario, Baye. In the surveys I asked both of you to fill out before meeting today, Teague mentioned she would like to design and install a chemical-free, environmentally friendly, waste-disposal system for the rescue center, so she becomes hyper-focused on this task. You're feeling irritable and jumpy. You tell her how you're feeling, but she is fixated on explaining her research regarding this disposal project. The technical aspects of the project make your eyes glaze over, but she can't redirect herself and insists that you should listen because she wants your input. You need her to back down and understand, but her disability keeps her from recognizing your escalating emotional state and concentrating on something else. She pushes you into a meltdown but doesn't realize she hasn't been listening to you and is the catalyst for your distress."

They were quiet. Both knew this could happen. Baye's thigh next to hers tensed, and her grip on Teague's hand loosened. Anxious that Baye might stand and leave the session, Teague began to slightly rock. The silence as Dr. Hansen watched them was loud, then deafening as the seconds ticked away. Teague's anxiety and rocking intensified until Dr. Hansen finally spoke again.

"So, what can we do? We can talk about ways to deescalate or even avoid this type of situation, but only if both of you are fully committed to making your relationship work."

When Baye slipped behind her on the sofa and wrapped her in a tight hug, Teague stilled and closed her eyes. "I know being with me can be difficult. My parents struggled with it. Connie has been the only one to understand…to stay with me." She placed her hands over Baye's arms, encouraging her hug. "Maybe I'm asking too much," she said.

"I could say the same, sweetheart. I'm so scared of disappointing you, terrified of hurting you," Baye said. "I've never seriously tried to manage my ADHD because I honestly enjoy the high from Adderall and self-medicating with marijuana. I hate the heavy mood-changing drugs doctors prescribe to even me out. My creativity goes silent when I'm on them. But I want to try if it means I can be with you. I love you, and I think we understand each other in a way no others can." She buried her face in Teague's neck and repeated. "I want to try more than anything."

Teague relaxed. "I want to try, too, because I want you to stay."

Dr. Hansen smiled. "Good. Although you might think I've been trying to dissuade you by pointing out how difficult this can be, I was only gauging your commitment to making this work. You have shown me today that you are determined and have an unusual connection. So, I'm very optimistic and hopeful I can help you both."

❖

Their bond felt deeper, stronger when they made love that night. They took their time, listening to their hearts as much as their bodies. Baye marveled again at Teague's transformation from her stiff and awkward girlfriend into her skilled, attentive lover. She was like a flower that bloomed when they touched skin-on-skin and caressed each other intimately. She gave herself wholly to Baye, then explored Baye's body with a confidence and enthusiasm that left her limp and panting from multiple orgasms.

Dr. Hansen's frank evaluation and assurance that their opposites-attract relationship could be successful had certainly fueled their connection and assuaged Baye's reticence about therapy. She was honest about her relationship with drugs. She refused to take the mood-altering drugs doctors had previously prescribed because they made her sluggish, and she sometimes abused Adderall because she liked the energy it gave her. She also habitually self-medicated by vaping cannabis. Dr. Hansen warned that she would not tolerate abuse of her Adderall prescription but promised she wouldn't prescribe the other drugs she disliked. People with ADHD were almost eight times more likely to use cannabis compared to those who didn't suffer from ADHD, she said. Those who did, however, often used the wrong strain. She gave her a prescription for a sativas strain of cannabis that had been shown to help mental conditions such as depression and ADHD. Dr. Hansen's willingness to work with her on a drug protocol lowered a huge hurdle for Baye.

When Baye spooned against the warmth of Teague's back, Teague guided her arm forward to tuck Baye's hand against her ribs, and their love settled over them like a blanket.

Yes. They could do this.

Chapter Eighteen

"Why do you brush your teeth before breakfast?" Teague struggled with Baye's morning routine, or lack of it. She sometimes showered before bed, and at other times, she showered in the mornings.

Baye rinsed her mouth, then gave Teague a minty kiss. "So I can do this."

"Oh. Okay." She couldn't argue with a kiss. The love and acceptance she absorbed from Baye was like nothing she'd felt before. Connie grounded her. She was her security, the mother figure who always had her back. Baye was a force that was widening her vision, at her side, and holding her hand as her world expanded with more real friends—Tommy, John, Libby, and maybe TJ. She could reach for Connie when she needed her, but Baye was a constant, comforting presence she could feel at the edge of her consciousness.

At Dr. Hansen's suggestion, Connie had explained to Baye some of Teague's peculiarities so she wouldn't stumble over them later. Libby, in turn, talked to Teague about some of the ADHD symptoms she could expect to encounter living with Baye. They also met with Dr. Hansen weekly to discuss their progress and attempt to anticipate future obstacles.

Connie smiled and placed Teague's ham-and-cheese omelet in front of her, along with a bowl containing four pieces of cantaloupe and three strawberries. "What would you like this morning, Baye?"

"I don't want to be any trouble. I can just have what Teague is having."

"Pretty, Pretty!" Mac called from the sunroom when he heard Baye's voice.

"Nonsense," Connie said, ignoring Mac's calls. "She might eat that every day for the next year, until she wakes up one morning and decides she wants a waffle. Then she'll eat that for the next year or more. You'll have to learn to ignore her repetitive habits and ask for what you want. Now, what do you want for breakfast?"

"Would a waffle with strawberries and whipped cream be too much trouble?"

"Not at all. In fact, that sounds so good, I think I'll have the same." She turned away to pull out her waffle iron and began gathering ingredients.

Teague poured coffee for each of them, then cut her omelet into sixteen precise pieces. "What are your plans for today?" she asked Baye.

"After I do my yoga, I'm going to work on the mural I'm painting in the cathouse between appointments with potential adopters. We have a family who lost their pit bull to old age and want to adopt another, a woman who is looking for a cat to keep her widowed mother company, and a young couple bringing their seven-year-old son to pick out his first dog."

"Your work must be so rewarding," Connie said. She placed a beautiful waffle in front of Baye and poured batter into the waffle iron for herself.

"It is. But it can be heartbreaking, too, when someone dumps off their ten-year-old dog because it's too old and has a medical problem they don't want to deal with, or we get an animal because their owner has died or lost their job so they can't afford to keep it any longer." She offered a bite of her waffle to Teague, who shook her head. "What's on your schedule today, sweetie?"

"I have a Zoom meeting this morning with the team that is developing a material with the density and tensile strength to withstand the heat of self-sustaining fusion when only centimeters thick," Teague said.

"I thought they were the people you spoke with in the middle of the night last week."

"No. Those people were in Japan. They are exploring alternative power sources to fusion. After the meeting, I will spend the afternoon calculating the possible mathematics of fusion power required to lift a small city—envision the *Enterprise* spaceship—past the earth's gravitational pull." Teague had learned to use fictional illustrations to help Connie and Baye better understand her work.

Baye patted her hand. "I'll wait for the movie."

Teague frowned. "We are not making a movie."

"It's an expression, dear," Connie said, smiling fondly at them. "It means the concept is too complicated for us to imagine, so we'll wait until it's a reality we can see."

Teague had come to understand that her work was too complicated for most to comprehend. She didn't mind, though, because she was happy enough to wage conversations and debate theories in her own head.

"You have time for your morning run before your meeting, right?" Baye gave her a pointed stare.

"Yes, dear," Teague said, giving her a quick kiss. "That is why I am wearing my running shorts."

"Good. Because Dr. Hansen said exercise is important for both of us, and I've noticed you're doing a lot less of that finger-tapping thing than you used to."

Connie pulled a small pillbox from the pocket of her apron and handed it to Baye. "And here's your morning medicine." They'd agreed to make Connie the dispenser of Baye's medicine so she didn't have to struggle with the temptation to abuse it.

"I'm feeling pretty good this morning. I might not need it."

"Dr. Hansen said you should take it every day at about the same time no matter how you feel," Teague said.

"Yes, dear." Baye teasingly mocked Teague's earlier phrase.

Connie and Baye laughed, and Teague managed a small smile. Laughter directed at her would normally throw her into a state of agitation, but she didn't mind their gentle teasing because she had learned it was not ridicule. Yes. She was growing now, rather than hiding from social interaction. And it felt good. Almost good enough to forget she would not live out the year.

❖

"How's it going?" Baye breezed into the farmhouse, still wearing her yoga pants and T-shirt. She felt good. Really good. Even though Dr. Hansen had slightly reduced her dosage of the medical cannabis, she still felt calm and clear-headed. She did miss sitting on the porch and vaping cannabis in the evening, but she and Teague had added a stroll around their properties each night that she found nearly as relaxing.

Libby and TJ looked up from their laptops, and both of them smiled.

"Pretty good," Libby said. "Our adoption numbers have nearly tripled this month since TJ has been keeping up with the applications and responding right away. She's doing a good job keeping the website current, too."

"I've got the numbers from the Find Your Best Friend weekend you arranged at the new dog park. We adopted out ten dogs and almost two dozen cats and kittens at the event, then five more the following week to people who went to the event, but waited for one reason or another to adopt," TJ said. "We actually have some empty dog runs for the first time this summer."

"That is so awesome. I think we have a winning team now," Baye said.

"Aren't you all sunshine today," Libby said. The comment held no hint of her cousin's usual sarcasm.

"So are you," Baye shot back.

"Libby has a boyfriend," TJ said.

Baye slapped her hand to her chest in dramatic surprise. "Tell me everything."

Libby flushed pink but smiled. "Remember the guy who came here two weeks ago, looking to adopt a pit bull?"

TJ cackled with laughter. "He went home with two chihuahuas and Libby's phone number."

"His name is Martin, and we've had two great dates. He's super sweet," Libby said.

"And—" Baye prodded for more.

"And a really good kisser."

TJ hooted, and Baye rounded the table to give her cousin a hug. "You look happy. I hope it works out."

"Me, too," Libby said, returning her hug. "Teague has been good for you, too." She kissed Baye's cheek. "I'm glad you're doing so much better."

"Looks like we're both doing better," she said.

This was true. Libby had lost her usual scowl and air of tension since their rescue center began to thrive.

The addition of Tommy had eased their worries about John lifting heavy things or handling overly energetic animals. Tommy was flourishing under John's gentle guidance, and John smiled a lot more since Tommy began living with him.

TJ also had been an excellent hire. They had taken over the work Baye had struggled with, which left her free to work where she excelled—event planning and meeting with adopters. Baye enjoyed talking with people as much as Teague avoided it. And event planning was her jam. She explained to Libby that she was able to overcome her short attention span by breaking down the planning into smaller bits—securing a location, food, entertainment, transportation logistics, and volunteer assignments. Also, Dr. Hansen encouraged her to make lists so she could circle back to tasks she left incomplete because of some distraction like an unrelated phone call. The chaos that had been her life was fading.

"Are you going to do anything with Teague's spreadsheets?" TJ asked.

And her bubble of happiness burst.

Teague couldn't die. She was Baye's lifeline, and they were just getting on their feet individually and relationship-wise. What's more, Baye loved all of Teague's animals, right down to the weird chicken with feathers on her feet. She didn't want to give any of them away.

"I've got a full schedule today. I'll take a look at them with you tomorrow." But she knew she wouldn't. She couldn't.

"Baye," Libby said gently. "Teague is paying us to rehome her pets. It's been two months, and you haven't placed even one. At some point, she's going to want to see some progress."

"I know." Damn. Her day had just gone from wonderful to the pits of despair. Her throat tightened as she looked up at Libby. "It's stupid anyway. She's not going to die. She just thinks she is." She straightened her shoulders. "Maybe I'll tell her to keep her money and stop her crazy obsession with a ridiculous family curse. I'll talk to Dr. Hansen and see if she can convince her it's not going to happen."

"I hope you're right, honey, but TJ's salary comes out of the money she's paying us. Heavy Petting is doing a lot better financially, but I'm not sure we can afford to keep paying TJ if you void our contract with Teague."

Baye exploded. "Damn it. I said I'd look at them tomorrow, okay?" She stomped out of the house and slammed the door.

❖

Eyes closed, Baye lay on the floor of the cat playroom, her chest vibrating with the purrs of a huge orange tomcat lying on her chest, and kittens playing with her fingers and in her hair. Tommy was cleaning the dog kennels, so she had a good cry in the small office of the cathouse and, when she found a vape pen she'd forgotten in the desk drawer, had a good smoke to chill out. That's exactly what she was doing now. Chilling.

She was roused from her drug-induced meditation by a knock on the glass picture window into the playroom.

"There you are," TJ said, opening the door to the playroom and speaking in a low voice. "You okay? I have Ms. Young and her mother with me. They're here to adopt one of our cats."

"I'm fine." Baye gently put the tomcat aside and stood. Her high was beginning to recede, and she'd had lots of practice functioning as normal when she was stoned.

TJ looked her over anxiously. "Your eyes are totally bloodshot."

She heaved a big sigh. TJ would see right through a lie. "I needed to chill, but it's wearing off already."

"Then can you help them? The couple looking for a pit bull was early. I left them with Tommy to show them the dogs, but I need to go handle the adoption of the dog they pick out."

She straightened her clothes, smoothed her hair, and smiled. "Sure." She loved showing off the cats. It was a perfect distraction.

❖

"You'll love this little cuddler." The older woman had picked out a petite, blue-eyed calico, whose spots were Siamese colors—chocolate, flame-point, and the blue-gray of a seal-point—rather than the more common orange, black, and white. "I think she's perfect for you."

"You're sure she's full grown? She's so small." The daughter cuddled the little cat before placing her in the carrier they'd brought.

"She was pregnant when she came to us but had only one

kitten. It was adopted earlier this month. So, she's at least a year old. She's neutered now, of course."

"I have a friend who has a Maine coon. That cat is huge, and she takes him with us on a leash when we go hiking together. It acts more like a dog than a cat. It rides in a kayak with her, and she has a backpack it sits in if the hike is too long and hot or we're near cars. It even wears a little life jacket when it rides in the kayak."

"Wow. I've never thought about taking a cat out in a boat, although I have heard of cats that like to swim." Baye handed over a cloth tote filled with several cat toys, the food they fed at the center, treat samples, some coupons from a local pet shop, and her vet records. They declined the offered litter and litter box because they'd already purchased one and decided where to place it in the woman's apartment. "Thank you for adopting and not buying from a breeder."

"Oh, we totally believe in adopting," the daughter said. "And we've heard good things about your rescue center."

"Thank you. You'll find several of our cards in your bag. Feel free to hand them out and recommend us to others who might need a canine or feline companion. They add so much to our lives," Baye said. She turned to the older Mrs. Young. "Now don't worry if she hides for a few days when you first take her home. Some of them do in a new place. Give her a little time, and she'll come out to explore. Then she'll be sitting in your lap and purring before you know it."

"Thank you, dear. We'll be fine. I had cats before I married, but my husband, God rest his soul, was allergic, so I haven't had one in years. I'm looking forward to spoiling this one."

TJ appeared just as they were walking toward their car and Baye was waving good-bye. "Your four o'clock appointment is here—the couple with the little boy."

Baye clapped her hands together, her earlier black mood forgotten. "Oh, goody. Helping him pick out a dog will be fun."

TJ looked relieved, handed Baye their paperwork, and

pointed to a young couple with a towheaded boy headed toward them. "I'll be in the house if you need me."

❖

Baye had spent nearly two hours with the couple and their little boy while they finally decided on a fifteen-pound, brown, rough-coat terrier, then completed the adoption paperwork. She was tired but happily surprised when she returned to the farmhouse and found Teague talking with TJ. She greeted Teague with a kiss and a heartfelt hug. "I missed you today."

Teague's expression lit up. "I came to a good stopping place early and thought I would come walk you home…to my house."

They'd moved about half of Baye's clothes to Teague's house, but neither had suggested they U-Haul the rest of her things. Teague's conviction that she would die in the next year precluded any final move. Her doctor had reported the ultrasound showed she had a strong, healthy heart, but the MRI had been bumped up again and was weeks away. Teague had suffered several severe headaches that her doctor insisted were not typical migraines, but hormone-induced headaches because they showed a pattern of happening the week before her menstrual period. Teague, of course, was not convinced.

"I was just asking TJ about your progress in rehoming my animals."

TJ said, "I told her that I'd finished the spreadsheets—"

Baye cut her off. "I've been looking over the spreadsheets a few hours every day and eliminating any you obviously wouldn't consider. But I've been pretty busy with painting the mural in the cathouse and helping people with adoptions. In fact, we had three adoptions this afternoon." She was babbling but couldn't seem to stop. She turned to TJ. "That little boy matched up with Sparky. You know, the little rough-coat terrier. Sparky acted like he'd known that boy all his life, and the boy fell in love with him right away."

Teague, true to her laser focus, persisted. “Have you found good candidates for any of them?”

TJ shrugged and gestured to Baye for her to answer.

“I have a good possibility for Leo. A woman who brought her mother here earlier today to adopt a cat said she hikes with a friend who has a Maine coon. She said the cat walks on a leash and goes with them. It even has a small lifejacket and rides in her friend’s kayak when they go camping. She said she’d like a Maine coon of her own to take along but said they’re too expensive even if she could find a breeder that wasn’t three states away. She might be perfect for Leo.” It was a small white lie built on a truth. The woman did mention the friend but had not expressed an interest in getting her own Maine coon.

Teague nodded. “Yes. Leo would hate to be cooped up in a house all the time. He needs to spend time outdoors in a way that is safe.”

“Wow. That sounds cool,” TJ said.

Baye had often spun tales to get herself out of trouble with her family and warmed to her storytelling. If only she’d stopped there.

“And, after looking over the people interested in the chickens, I narrowed it down to a woman who just bought an old farmhouse out in the country. She said the property has a barn, and she has been looking at plans for building a chicken coop in it.”

“My hens are past their prime and have laid only a few eggs recently.”

“I pointed that out, and she said she’s single and doesn’t need a lot. She said she had a pet chicken when she was a child but has never lived in a place where she could have chickens again. Her company lets her work remotely since the pandemic, so she was able to move out to the country again.” Okay. That was a total fabrication.

She glanced at TJ, who had narrowed their eyes in suspicion, and gave a nearly imperceptible shake of her head. She knew

Baye hadn't even looked at the spreadsheets, much less called any of the applicants.

"Perhaps she would be interested in the rabbits, too," Teague said, nodding her approval.

"Oh, I hadn't thought of that," Baye said. "She might, especially if she saw how beautiful they are." Okay. Time to shut up, because she was digging herself into a hole. What if Teague wanted the woman to come meet the rabbits, or asked to visit this fictional woman's farm to check out her accommodations for Miss Henny and her girls? "I still have to check her references and make sure she really does have a farm. Right now, I'm starving. I just want to forget about business for today, have dinner with you and Connie, take our evening stroll, and spend some time with the fur kids." She took Teague's arm and guided her to the door. "And most of all, I want to spend some time with my handsome escort."

Chapter Nineteen

Teague stepped back from the whiteboard and closed her eyes. The sharp, throbbing pain started at her nape and curled over the top of her head and around through her right temple. She had been trying to ignore the headache, but it had grown to the point she was nauseous and the daylight coming through the tall windows felt as though it was burning her retinas.

"I am sorry, but I must continue this meeting at another time," she said to the three scientists on the teleconference. Without waiting for them to sign off, she closed the app and opened a new one. "Computer, call Dr. Brennen from my personal contacts."

"Dr. Brennen's office, this is Lisa."

"This is Teague Maxwell. I need to speak with Dr. Brennen."

"I'm sorry, Ms. Maxwell. He's with a patient right now."

"Where is Susan?" Dr. Brennan's personal nurse knew her and would get Dr. Brennen on the phone.

"Susan is on vacation this week. I'm filling in as Dr. Brennen's nurse while she's out. I can give him a message when he's free, but he's booked solid today. Do you want me to transfer you to appointment scheduling?"

Teague began to rock back and forth, but the repetitive motion increased her nausea rather than calmed her. "I need to speak to him now." She grasped her head, immediately regretting that she had shouted. The pain was drowning out any coherent thought. She lowered her volume. "This is Teague Maxwell. I think my brain is bleeding. Tell him now."

"If you are having an emergency, Ms. Maxwell, you should hang up and call nine-one-one or go to the emergency room."

She slashed her hand across the computer to swipe the icon ending the call.

Snow left his bed in the cottage and pressed against her legs for support. Agitated by her raised voice, Cappie skittered away, overturning Snow's metal water bowl, which clattered against the tiled floor. Mac paced on his perch and screeched. "Call the doctor. Call the doctor."

She sank to the floor and curled into herself, closing her eyes and covering her ears.

"Teague. Baby, what's wrong?" Baye was bent over Teague, rubbing her back. "Another headache?"

"Yes." She could barely whisper.

"Call the doctor. Call the doctor," Mac screamed.

"Mac, shush. Whisper. Inside voice." Baye whispered to demonstrate.

The macaw cocked his head and responded with a hoarse stage whisper. "Whisper. Inside voice."

"Honey, can you stand? I need to get you into the house. Don't open your eyes. I'll guide you."

"Might throw up."

"That's okay if you need to." Baye punched a speed dial and whispered into her phone. "Connie. Teague is having one of those migraines. Can you ask the cleaning people to go and come back another day. Their vacuum noise and cleaning smells won't be good for her…Yeah, I'm going to bring her up from the cottage…Thanks."

Teague's head spun as Baye helped her stand and walked her into the house. She managed to keep her breakfast from coming back up and sighed in relief when she lay down in her bedroom Connie had already darkened and cooled several degrees below its normal temperature.

"MRI," Teague whispered. "I need to get that MRI."

Baye administered the single-dose injection of pain medicine prescribed by her doctor, and the pain began to ease its grip on her skull.

"My animals," she mumbled. "Not ready."

"Sleep," Baye said quietly, and then, with a light kiss to her forehead, faded into the dark.

❖

"Wow. Your mural looks really great," TJ said. "Did you major in art at college?"

Baye stepped back and decided a touch more of gray should go on the kitten who was batting a feather toy. "No. I never stayed at college long enough to declare a major. I just couldn't sit through those long classes and spend an entire night cramming for a test."

"I'd think the art classes would be interesting."

"You would think so, but they were really regimented. The teacher would make the whole class paint the same apple in a bowl or the sun on the horizon. When they started talking about technique and special perspective and stuff, my eyes glazed over. I just paint what I see and feel in my head."

TJ seemed to consider this information as they watched Baye work. "Sort of like a musician that doesn't read music but can play anything if they hear it once." Then they laughed. "I guess that's how Flower paints, too."

While the wall in the adoption room of the cathouse was Baye's canvas, Flower was creating her own art next to her on a twelve-by-twenty-inch canvas clamped to a floor-level easel.

Flower turned those dark pig eyes on TJ, then took a moment to look at her canvas and spit out the brush she held in her mouth to select a brush filled with a different color for her next strokes. She took her art very seriously.

When Baye had discovered the pig had definite color preferences, she made a series of color swatches of the tempera paints she had available and spread them on the floor. Flower would select from the swatches by pushing them toward Baye with her nose, and then Baye would mix the paints in cans that had previously held bulk vegetables and put a brush in each one. Flower would paint one color at a time, taking the brush from the color she wanted in her mouth and slashing it across the canvas. The astonishing thing was that Flower's selection of color and her paint strokes were obviously purposeful, not random.

"You could learn something from her color selection," Baye said. She couldn't bring herself to sort through the offers to rehome Flower, because she felt a kinship to the little pig. People judged them both too often by what they saw on the outside.

"So, have you looked at the applicants I highlighted on the spreadsheets?" TJ asked carefully. She had definitely figured out that rehoming Teague's pets was a sore subject with Baye.

A handful of people had applied to take Lucky or Asset. Only one was a working farm that needed a guard animal. Several were seeking a companion for a llama or donkey they already had. The farm might be suitable for Lucky, but their herd was a large one in a remote pasture. Asset loved people and would be lonely living with a bunch of sheep and a couple of llamas. He needed human interaction, too.

Maybe Teague would reconsider her refusal to consider a petting-zoo situation, at least where Asset was concerned.

A couple who had established a brush-clearing-goats-for-hire business was interested in Snow. They often camped in a small trailer when they were at a location several days or weeks while their goats ate away at forest undergrowth or a neglected pasture a farmer wanted to reclaim. They would use Snow to help guard the herd at night, just as he did for Teague. They also offered to take the goats, but not the sheep, which were picky about what they ate.

"The goat people look like a good possibility, but I'd have

to meet with them," Baye said. "Teague might also want to, and she's super busy right now with her collider project."

"Did you see the entry on the organic farmers? They would be a great possibility for the chickens. They let their chickens free-range to eat the bugs from their summer and winter gardens."

"Chickens are mean. If the people already have an established flock, their chickens will probably pick on Miss Hennie and her girls. None of them are very big hens. An established flock will peck and peck at the newcomers until they draw blood, and sometimes even kill them. It makes me want to cry to think about some bitch hen hurting sweet Miss Hennie. We need to find somebody who doesn't already have a flock."

TJ was quiet for a long time, watching as Baye and Flower painted. She finally spoke quietly. "You and Libby signed a contract, Baye. You and Teague becoming lovers doesn't void a legal contract unless Teague agrees to break it. I don't think she's going to do that."

Baye sighed and put down her brush. The mural was finished, and she continued to tweak it simply to avoid the rehoming project. Honestly, she was attached to every one of those animals. She loved it when Mac called out, "Pretty. Here's Pretty," when he heard her voice. She wanted to paint lots of pictures with Flower. It made her feel good when Cappie chose her shoulder to snuggle on while she and Teague watched a movie. And the little brooding sound Miss Hennie made when Baye held her in her lap and stroked her was very soothing.

Still, none of that was the real reason she was putting off rehoming these animals she'd come to feel were as much hers as Teague's. Deep inside, she had an unfounded feeling that Teague wouldn't die as long as some of them still needed good homes.

Chapter Twenty

The ride was silent.

They'd loaded Abigail, Tater, and Tot into a small horse trailer and Snow into the back seat of the crew-cab truck Teague had borrowed from Mary Anne Beck, and Teague was driving the first of her crew to their new family—the couple with the brush-eating goats.

The severity of her last headache had filled her with a sense of urgency. She needed to know her animals were going to good homes. The next headache could be her last.

Teague had thought Baye would argue against the many stipulations—some a little unrealistic—she'd laid down for rehoming her pets, but it was Baye who resisted this first placement. Abigail and her kids were used to eating lush pasture grass, supplemented daily with high-grade pellets, Baye argued. They had a pond and a trough for plenty of fresh water. What if they were taken to a location without adequate water?

But they'd met with the couple, and all questions were answered to Teague's satisfaction. Any remaining doubts vanished when they pulled into a neat, small farm with a freshly painted barn and several large, grassy paddocks.

"This looks good," Teague said.

Baye didn't answer but picked up Snow's leash and exited the truck.

The couple met them in the circular drive.

"Hi. I hope you didn't have any trouble finding the place."

"We did not. I used the truck's GPS system."

TJ had prepped the couple over the phone before their first meeting, so they knew not to offer a handshake or to take offense when Teague spoke without meeting their eyes. The woman, Kathy, had grown up on a farm that had dairy goats, so she was familiar with what was required to keep a herd healthy. Jimmy, her husband, was a beanpole of a man, with a bushy beard that nearly touched his T-shirt collar. He was raised in the suburbs but enthusiastic about adopting his wife's back-to-basics lifestyle. After college, they agreed they didn't want to join the corporate rat race, so they started their successful goat business.

Teague was surprised that Baye hung back. She was normally the social one, smiling and immediately striking up conversations with almost any stranger. She finally joined them with Snow at her side.

A medium-sized black dog with a white chest raced out from the barn when she spotted Snow. The big dog stood tall and swished his feathery tail back and forth as they sniffed each other.

"This is Tessie," Kathy said. "Somebody dumped her out at the end of the road when she was just a pup. She showed up here hungry and scared, and she's never left."

"Best dog ever," Jimmy said. "She keeps rodents out of the barn."

"We just acquired a young doe with triplets about the same age as your kids. She's a little shy, so we thought we'd put her and Abigail in the paddock on the left and let them get to know each other. Since Abigail is older and still has her horns, we're hoping she'll take this young mother under her wing and keep any of the other goats from picking on her when we finally mix them with the main herd."

Baye spoke for the first time. "What if the other goats pick on Abigail? I can come back and get them if they don't work out."

Kathy smiled. "We expect that Abigail will become the boss of the herd. We don't breed our goats, so they are all does or neutered bucks. At her age and being the only goat with horns, she'll rank high in their pecking order or, at the very least, let them know she's not to be bothered. She'll be fine."

Jimmy knelt before Snow and ruffled his shaggy shoulders. "Hey, boy. We're sure glad to have you with us." He looked up at Baye. "He'll be a big help, watching over the goats when we go out on a job."

"He normally stays out with the goats at night," Teague said. She was glad he would have a dog friend because she didn't want him to miss Badger too much.

"We've got a nice bed in the barn for him, but he's also welcome to sleep in the house with us if he wants," Kathy said. "You can let him loose, and we'll get the goats into the pasture."

Snow, with his new friend in tow, went over to check out the main herd.

Abigail and the kids hopped down from the trailer when Teague opened it. Several of the other goats in the paddock to the right came to the fence to have a look at the newcomers. Abigail gave them a stare and a flip of her tail, then followed Teague to her own paddock. The smaller, white goat watched nervously as Abigail eyed her, but the kids instantly bounded toward each other and began playing after only a cursory hello. Abigail began to graze, and the younger doe moved closer to graze with her.

They watched the goats as Snow entered the paddock and stood so the new kids could check him out. They were climbing over him in no time, and their nervous mother went back to grazing when she saw Abigail wasn't concerned about the big dog.

"See?" Kathy said. "They're going to be fine."

"That is good," Teague said. "We have to return the trailer, so we should go."

Baye went to Snow and hugged him for a long moment, then went to the truck without saying good-bye.

"Is she okay?" Kathy asked.

"She is emotional," Teague said, explaining Baye's departure as best she could. "Thank you for giving them a good home. Their vet records should be in your email."

Baye didn't say anything when Teague climbed into the truck but began to sob when Snow realized they were leaving and Jimmy had to grab his collar and hold him back from following. She went straight to Teague's Jeep when they returned the truck to Mary Anne. Teague thanked Mary Anne, then joined Baye in the Jeep.

"I don't know how you can be so cold about this," Baye said, tears still running down her face.

Teague handed her a tissue from a box in the console. "I am relieved that Snow and my goats will have a good home. They are good people, and knowledgeable about how to care for them. They have new friends now, too." She placed her hand tentatively on Baye's thigh. "I would not want to die and have one of my relatives send them to the auction yard. It is the right thing to do."

Baye looked out the window, and their ride again was silent.

❖

Baye stared at the ceiling of her bedroom. Her bedroom. She told Teague she needed some space to think and stayed at the farmhouse for the first time in a month. She ignored TJ and Libby, went straight to her bedroom, rummaged in her dresser for her last vape pen, and closed the blinds to lie in the dark and shut out the world. Life was too mean. She felt things too deeply.

She twirled the pen in her fingers but didn't put it to her lips. This was what she'd always done, hidden in a cannabis haze so she didn't have to feel. So, why was she hesitating now? The medical cannabis and Adderall adjustment had worked for her. She felt calm, yet still creative. She still had to make an effort to focus, but the exercise and regular meals that Connie cooked for them had evened her keel. Then there was Teague. Sweet, practical Teague. She was so many things—so intelligent and knowledgeable, but endearingly awkward and socially naive, and, contrary to her handicap, an attentive and adept lover.

Baye put the pen aside. Teague was not going to die on her. That curse thing, no matter how unreasonably convinced Teague seemed, was just plain stupid.

So, instead of retreating to a drugged bliss, she began to make a plan.

Chapter Twenty-one

"Well, hey. You're just in time for breakfast." Connie's greeting was cheerful but cautious.

Teague looked up from her breakfast—her usual ham, egg, and cheese omelet, with fruit on the side. She'd found it impossible to sleep. She missed the rhythm of Baye's light snores. She'd given up and gone to the cottage to work, but even the siren of numbers and symbols failed to entrance her. She'd ended up walking the path she and Baye strolled each evening…the part that was on her property. She was afraid she'd wake the dogs if she made the entire loop that wound near the kennels. Finally, she'd returned to bed and slept two fitful hours before rising. She wasn't even hungry but was eating her breakfast anyway in the hope routine would again balance her world left off-kilter by Baye's absence.

She hesitated when Baye came to her and wordlessly opened her arms, then stood and relaxed into her long, firm hug. When Baye released her, she took Teague's face in her soft hands and brushed their lips together.

"I'm sorry. I needed some time alone to get my emotions under control. I know it's hard for you to understand, but this was something I needed to do without your help."

Teague did understand. "Are you okay? Should you go talk to Dr. Hansen?"

"I'm fine now. We can discuss it when we go for our monthly appointment in two weeks." Baye took her usual seat at the kitchen island. "You know what? I'll have exactly what she's having."

Connie's smile was relaxed and genuine this time. "Coming right up."

"I missed your snoring last night," she said to Teague.

Teague narrowed her eyes at Baye. "I do not snore, but you do." Then she smiled. "And I missed your snores, too."

❖

"I have to fly to NASA in Washington next week," Teague said.

"Oh, no. I'm not ready to spend another night without you." She really wasn't. They'd fallen asleep tangled in each other's arms every night since Baye had stayed at her house that one time.

"Ask Connie to let Badger sleep with you. He snores."

Baye slapped Teague's arm playfully as they walked their evening route. If she didn't know better, she'd swear Teague was developing a sense of humor. "How long will you be gone?" The day was warm, and the cool radiating up as they rounded the pond felt wonderful.

Teague frowned. "Four days. I hate to travel, but Dr. Turner needs me to attend several meetings that will secure our project's funding for the next few years. The German team is flying in so we can discuss their progress face-to-face."

She entwined her fingers with Teague's as they walked. "I'll miss you terribly. We should eat breakfast together every morning on a video call. And you have to call again to say good night, or I won't be able to sleep."

"Yes. Dr. Turner is familiar with my needs, so he does everything he can to make me comfortable when I have to visit. But setting up times to talk each day will help." Teague brought their joined hands to her lips and kissed the back of Baye's. Teague rarely initiated affection between them, so Baye knew she was very pleased with this idea. Teague's absence would also give Baye a chance to initiate her plan.

❖

"Mary Anne, thank you so much for doing this." The Fluffies—Cotton, Crochet, and Yarn—were already grazing while Lucky surveyed their new pasture.

"I like Teague. I grew up with an autistic cousin, so her quirks don't bother me. I miss her coming over for a ride every couple of months."

"Hopefully, she won't decide to do that while Lucky and the sheep are here."

"Like I said, if the sheep eat that field down to the roots, it's okay. I'm planning to cut those pines at the other end and have that field graded and sand hauled in to make another outdoor ring. That gives you until a month after Teague's forty-first birthday. After that, you're going to have to take them back or find a permanent home for them somewhere else."

"Gotcha. Hopefully, she'll forget about that ridiculous family curse after her next birthday."

The first part of her plan in place, Baye happily drove to her next stop.

❖

"Hello, Miss Flower. Aren't you pretty with your little bow around your neck. Y'all come inside. It's so hot today." The elderly lady held the sliding glass door open for Flower to enter.

Baye was ecstatic when Mrs. Kowalczyk applied for Flower. She and her husband had recently lost their pet pig to snout cancer, so they already had the knowledge and all the things needed to keep Flower happy and healthy. When she called them,

Mrs. Kowalczyk said she was sorry, but they spent every winter in Florida and had decided after they put in the application that since they were getting older, traveling with a pig was more than they wanted to deal with again. "Thank you so much for fostering Flower for us. I know you guys are leaving in the fall, but I just need a place for her until October."

"That's perfect for us, dear. We'll be here through Thanksgiving to spend it with our children and the grandkids, and then we hit the road for Florida until we come back in April."

"She's great on a leash and loves to watch cartoons. I brought her paints, too."

"Oh. John can't wait to see her paint. He wants to set her up on the patio for an art session as soon as she feels settled in. We miss Rosy so much that fostering Flower is going to ease our grieving. You know, it's like losing a family member."

"Oh, I know. I'll call from time to time if you don't mind, to see how she's doing. And you can call me anytime if you have any questions about her."

"We'll be fine. And you're welcome to visit her if you want."

"We stay pretty busy at the rescue center, so I'll keep in touch, but I don't know that I'll get a chance to visit."

"Well, you don't have to worry. She'll do fine."

❖

Several applicants wanted the rabbits for breeding, but they both had been neutered. Several more wanted just one rabbit and weren't willing to give them up if they got them. She finally found a heritage farm where the owner specialized in old breeds of farm animals. The farm hosted school groups during the year for educational tours. It wasn't a petting zoo that had constant visitors, which Teague felt could stress the animals. Since they were a breeding farm, they agreed to basically board the rabbits and Asset until October. They were only asking for enough to cover the animals' food and treats, so Baye agreed. She'd pay it out of her personal account since she had extra these days. She still split the farmhouse utilities with Libby because TJ was saving up for the next school year, but Teague refused to let her contribute to the grocery bill or pay very often if they ordered takeout.

❖

Cappie and Mac were tougher. Baye had grown very attached to the little capuchin monkey and the raucous macaw, and none of the few who applied to rehome them were acceptable in her eyes. She planned to talk to Teague again about letting her take them if her family curse proved real.

But she couldn't think about that now. She knew in her heart it wouldn't happen. If there was a god, he surely wouldn't be cruel enough to take such a sweet, brilliant woman from her. Her confidence that Teague would survive her forty-first birthday fueled her mission to arrange temporary homes for their animal family. She had even worked out a plausible story for where Lucky and the sheep were placed and the excuse she'd give Teague for placing them while she was away without a chance to say good-bye.

Today, she was sketching a mural for the kennel adoption room, since the one in the cathouse had drawn so many compliments. Yep. Everything was great. They'd talked twice a day while Teague was gone, and she was getting ready to leave for the airport now to pick her up. Connie would be at her church's bingo night, so they'd have the house to themselves. She couldn't wait.

❖

Baye pulled Teague on top of her. God, it seemed like forever since she'd felt her soft, warm skin against her own. Legs spread wide, she wrapped her legs around Teague's hips. She reached down to part both their sexes, wet and slick from delayed gratification. Teague began to thrust. "That's right, baby. Feels so good. I missed you, I missed this. I am so hard for you." She skated her hands down Teague's long, smooth back and gripped her buttocks to coax her to thrust with a firmer stroke.

"I feel it." Teague's voice was hoarse and strained.

She felt it too—the gathering of desire in her belly, the indescribable twinge in her clit as Teague's raked it. "Yes. Like that. Come on, baby. I'm going to come."

Teague stiffened and growled, pumping harder and faster against her until she exploded with a cry, digging her nails into Teague's back and riding the waves of sensation as her thrusts slowed, then finally stopped.

"I love you," she said. She didn't expect Teague to say it back. She rarely voiced what she showed her in every fleeting glance and shy touch. Some would find Teague's difficulty to recognize and express emotion too much for their fragile self-confidence. Baye should have felt the same, since she struggled to love her ADHD self, but she didn't. Instead, Teague was her anchor. She was incapable of lies and deception. She had no filter in her conversations and actions, which meant she would never say anything behind anyone's back that she wouldn't say to their face. That was a wonderful quality, not a handicap, in Baye's estimation, that few others possessed.

Teague kissed her, then rolled them so that she was the big spoon for a change, snaking an arm around Baye's ribs and molding her body against Baye's…holding on like she was afraid Baye would leave.

"Always," Baye whispered, reveling in Teague's affirming squeeze.

Chapter Twenty-two

Teague ran the loop around their joint property for the fourth time, then slowed to a walk to cool down. She didn't mind that Baye disliked running. She enjoyed, craved every minute they spent together, but it was a big change from her relatively isolated life before. She still needed a little alone time to rattle around in her own head, and the rhythmic slap of her feet on the path set a soothing tone for the rest of her day.

When she reached her property again, she walked to the barn rather than the house. Baye had told her the animals were gone.

"You might not show it or even recognize it, but, deep down inside, Snow trying to follow when we left hurt you as much or more than it did me," Baye had said. "I wanted to spare you the good-byes and give myself time to handle my feelings before you got back."

Baye's explanation made sense, but she didn't really know what to do with the hollow feeling in her chest when she looked at the empty stalls and pasture. She missed Asset's braying run anytime he saw her and watching Tater and Tot scamper around the others, rebounding off their backs chasing each other. She wished Snow was there to lay his big head in her lap for an ear scratch, while Miss Hennie and her girls clucked pleasantly as they scratched and pecked the ground for tasty insects and worms.

It was for the best, she told herself. Her time was growing

short, less than two months until her birthday. Her MRI was scheduled for later in the week, but she had a sense of approaching doom that she didn't think even a good report could appease.

She started for the house, then decided she needed an extra dose of the one person who could fill all her hollow places, and instead, turned toward the farmhouse.

❖

Baye was in such good spirits, she practically bounced through the back door of the farmhouse.

"Whoa. Somebody's in a good mood," TJ said. "And I'm about to make it better."

"You can't possibly," she said, retrieving a bottle of water from the refrigerator. She was bursting with energy after her night with Teague, breakfast, then yoga. She loved her life right now.

"You got a call from a woman who saw one of your birthday party flyers and wants to talk with you." She held out a pink Sticky Note. "This is her number. She said you can call in the mornings between ten and noon. I told her I didn't think that would be a problem."

"Awesome," Baye said. She broke out into a brief happy dance, then stopped mid-hop when TJ's expression changed. "What?"

"You should talk to Tommy and try to cheer him up. He worships you, and he's very sad that he has only Mac and Cappie to take care of at Teague's place. John says he still goes over there with Buster and sits in the empty barn."

Baye sighed. "I know. It breaks my heart to go in that barn myself. I just don't know how to explain to him that Teague is convinced she's going to die, and the animals will be coming back when she doesn't. He's an open book, and I know he'd let the secret slip when he's around Teague."

TJ closed her laptop and stared at Baye. "I know you're

happy about finding temporary places for her animals, but this whole thing could blow up in your face, you know."

"It won't. I won't let it."

"I hope so. You know her better than I do. But if I were you, I'd be afraid your deception will damage the trust between you two."

"She'll be so glad when I bring them home after her birthday that she won't even think about the little lie I've told."

"What about ones still there—Leo, Cappie, and Mac?"

"I'm still trying to convince Teague to let me have Cappie and Mac. I have some ideas for winning her over on that subject. Leo has a dozen good applicants, but none of them want to just foster him and give him up. I'm still looking for a temporary home for him."

"Why not just place him permanently?"

"He sleeps on the bed with us most nights. When we watch television, Cappie cuddles on my shoulder, and Leo drapes himself across her lap. She'd miss him too much if I rehomed him."

"What are you going to do when she pushes you to go ahead and find a home for him? She's seen how many applicants were on his spreadsheet. You've already lied to her about finding a woman who would take him hiking and kayaking with her. She'll want to meet her and place Leo right away. You know, snatch the Band-Aid off all at once."

"Don't you worry about it."

"I do worry. I like Teague, and you're lying to her about the animals." TJ's voice rose when Baye turned and went back into the kitchen to get away from the things she didn't want to think about. "What if this family curse is real? Or maybe she believes it enough that she really will pop an aneurysm thinking about it? What are you going to do if she does die, and you have to find permanent homes for them?"

"Stop it." Baye was back at the table where TJ was working

in three fast strides. She shouted back. "Just stop it. Teague is not going to die. She will understand I tricked her because I don't want her to lose the animals she loves. The fur babies I love now, too. She's not going to die, and I'm going to get them all back when she doesn't, and she'll understand."

"Uh, Baye."

She whirled toward the front door where Libby stood with Teague right behind her. Teague's face was blank, but her hand tapped a nervous pattern against her hip.

Baye's heart dropped. How much had she heard? "Teague, baby."

Teague turned and strode out the door. Baye scrambled to follow, but she had hopped the fence and was running across the pasture now.

"Shit."

"She was standing on the porch about to knock when I got here, so she just came in with me," Libby said, her words weak and tentative.

Baye turned back to TJ and pointed at her. "This is your fault. What I did with her animals is none of your business. Now look what you've done." She was screaming. She was losing it. "You're fired. Get your stuff and go." She headed for the door.

"Where are you going?" Libby stepped aside to get out of her path.

"To find Teague and fix this."

❖

Teague locked the door to the cottage and lowered the shades to darken the entire room. Baye had lied to her. She couldn't see it. She couldn't read the deception. What else had she lied about? Would she continue to lie?

Uncertainty tore at her, and rage filled her. She looked at the numbers on her whiteboard. Maybe they were a lie, too. She threw all but one marker across the room, scattering them everywhere, then used the remaining one to draw long, slashing marks and scribbles over the equation she'd worked on for weeks. She could trust nothing.

She willed her aorta or the vessels in her brain to burst. All her pain would go away in minutes. She prayed to whatever higher power might be to take her into blessed, final darkness.

Banging, banging, banging on the door enraged her even more.

"Teague, honey. Let me explain."

"No, no, no," she screamed. She grabbed her desk and heaved it over, shattering the glass top. "You lied. Leave me alone. You lied to me."

"Oh my God. What was that? Oh my God. Are you hurt?"

"Go away." She yelled so loud her throat hurt.

"Please Teague. Let me explain. I love you. I didn't mean to hurt you. Let me in, Teague. Please don't hurt yourself."

Teague left the main room and went in to the windowless, small bedroom of the cottage. She locked the door and curled into a fetal position on the bed. Her head hurt. Her chest hurt. Baye's betrayal hurt so bad.

❖

Baye ran to the house where Connie was in the kitchen.

"Come quick. Teague is having a major breakdown in the cottage. She won't let me in, and I can hear her breaking things."

Connie looked up, her eyes wide. "What in the world? What happened?"

"She was upset by something she overheard, then ran off and locked herself in the cottage."

"Oh, dear. She hasn't thrown things since she was a child." She pulled a ring of house keys from the pocket of her dress and hurried into the pantry. "I better get a sedative to calm her down." She used the keys to open a locked drawer and took out one of two injector pens. "I hope these are still good. It's been so long since she's had a freak-out. I normally keep these up to date, but she's been doing so well, I hadn't even thought of it. This one has just expired. You better come with me. I might need help restraining her."

❖

Connie knocked on the door of the cottage. It was quiet inside now. "Teague? Honey? Let me in, okay?"

No answer.

"There was a big crash," Baye said. "I could hear glass shattering. She might be hurt."

Connie pulled her keys out again and unlocked the door, opening it cautiously. No Teague, but the room was a wreck. The glass-top desk was in a million pieces, but Baye didn't see any blood.

"She's probably in the bedroom," Connie said. She went to the closed door and knocked. "Teague? Are you okay?"

No answer again.

Baye was scared. She had no idea Teague was capable of the destruction she saw in the main room.

Connie used her keys again, unlocking the bedroom door. "Honey, Baye's here. Whatever's wrong, we can work it out, okay?"

"No, no. She lied."

Baye flinched at the shriek, and something hit the door. Another loud bang, but away from the door.

Connie squared her shoulders. "Let me go in. I'll yell if I need you." She slipped past the door and closed it.

Baye could hear the murmur of voices—Teague's sharp tones mixed with Connie's soothing alto. Another bang, then more voices. It seemed like a lifetime before Connie finally opened the door. Baye could see Teague curled up on the bed, her back to the door.

Connie closed it quietly. "I gave her the shot. She'll sleep probably for the next eight to ten hours if that injection hasn't lost its potency."

"How often does this happen?" Baye asked.

"I don't think I've seen her so bad she tore stuff up since she was a child. I keep the shots up to date because she would sometimes work without sleeping for several days, and I'd have to force her to rest, then eat." Connie led her out of the cottage. "I'll call the agency to get this cleaned up, and I'll check in on her periodically until she wakes up."

"I can stay with her."

Connie patted her on the arm. "I don't think that's wise, honey. Just the mention of your name set her off again. She's punched a couple of holes in the bedroom wall. I'll have to get some repairmen in later, but we should leave her alone for now."

"This is TJ's fault. She should mind her own business."

"Can you tell me what happened?"

Baye confessed it all—her deception and Teague walking in while TJ was talking about it.

Connie shook her head. "You can't blame TJ, honey. This is something you did, and you need to take that responsibility so you won't ever do it again if she gives you another chance."

"If?"

"You must realize all that Teague has overcome. The one thing she hasn't been able to master is being able to read people. She's been taken advantage of in many situations because she's incapable of lying or deception, so she can't begin to anticipate or recognize that trait in other people. She was hard to raise because you couldn't tell her the little stories you normally tell children about a tooth fairy or the Easter bunny. Lying is her deal-breaker."

"How do I make this right, Connie?"

"I don't know, dear. Give her time. I'll talk to her tomorrow and get her to go see Dr. Hansen, but you shouldn't pressure her. It could set her back again. You should go home and let me handle this."

Chapter Twenty-three

"Baye, you've got to stop this now." Libby came into her darkened bedroom and opened the light-blocking drapes. "You've been holed up in here without eating or bathing for four days. You haven't taken your medicine or done your yoga. Enough is enough."

Baye had waited three days, existing on nothing but Connie's covert updates. Teague was okay, but she refused to talk to Connie about what had happened. She had been working in her suite of rooms until a new desk arrived and the whiteboard that she'd pounded with her desk chair was replaced. But then Tommy had showed up with all of Baye's things packed in a couple of boxes. Teague was done with her. Baye sank into a well of depression and hadn't left her bedroom in over a week.

"I can't. I can't fix this, and I can't live with it."

"You're starting to scare me. Either you get up and take a shower and come downstairs to eat something, or I'm going to call Dr. Hansen and tell her you might be suicidal."

"I can't get up."

"Then I'm going to get TJ, and we'll pick you up and put you in the shower."

"I fired TJ."

"No, you didn't. Human resources falls under my duties, and I unfired them."

Baye sat up in the bed, squinting when Libby turned on the bedside light. "Can you tell them I'm sorry?"

Libby handed her some pills and a glass of water. "Take these. No argument or I'll call Dr. Hansen."

She swallowed the pills and started to lie back again, but Libby grabbed her hand and pulled her up, then led her to the bathroom. "You can tell them when you come downstairs after you shower. Then we can talk about a plan for what to do next. I'll go get you some clean clothes."

❖

"I don't know what to do, Dr. Hansen." Baye grabbed another tissue. She was so tired of crying, but she felt she was at the bottom of a deep well with no way to get out. "She won't even talk to me. I never meant to hurt her. I wanted to save her animals for her. She loves them so much."

"You have to understand that Teague sees almost everything as black and white. There are no gray areas for her. She believed you understood her handicap and would safeguard it. Instead, she thinks you knowingly took advantage of her inability to recognize deceit when you lied to her."

"I didn't. I didn't realize."

Dr. Hansen's secretary stepped into the office after a quick knock at the door. "I'm so sorry to interrupt, Dr. Hansen, but there is an emergency at the hospital. I know Ms. Cobb usually comes in with Ms. Maxwell, and the emergency involves Ms. Maxwell."

"Oh my God. Teague's in the hospital?" Baye jumped to her feet.

"I don't know the circumstances, but they asked if you could come right away," the secretary said.

"Yes," Dr. Hansen said, rising. "I'll go now."

Baye's phone rang. It was Connie. "Connie, are you with Teague?"

"No. I'm sitting with my sister's grandchildren while she's at a dentist appointment. The hospital called me because I'm Teague's emergency contact, but I can't leave. The children are napping. It would take me too long to wake them and get to the hospital. Can you go?"

"I'm with Dr. Hansen, and they just called her. Her office is in a building next to the hospital. We're going over there now."

"She's been so fragile lately. She insisted she could go alone for the MRI, but she's apparently having an episode because she doesn't do well in tight places, and they don't know what to do."

Baye followed Dr. Hansen as they hurried through the skywalk connecting the medical office building with the hospital. "We're on our way. I'll call you after we get her calmed down."

"I'm not sure seeing you will help, Baye. You should let me handle this," Dr. Hansen said.

"I love her, and she's in pain. If I make it worse, I'll leave, but you can't stop me from seeing her."

When they reached the MRI suite, a technician greeted them. "Are you Dr. Hansen?"

"Yes. Where's Ms. Maxwell?"

The technician pointed to a door. "She's in the MRI room, but she's freaking out and won't let anyone touch her. I called security. They might have to hold her so you can sedate her."

"Don't let them in. Let me see what I can do first. Do you have a sedative?"

"Yes. A lot of patients request it for the full-body scans because they take so long."

"Give it to me." She slipped the syringe in her blazer's pocket and turned to Baye. "You can come in, but if she reacts badly to seeing you, I want you to leave immediately."

Baye nodded but didn't promise.

When they stepped inside, Teague was raging, pacing back and forth. She was dressed in sweatpants and a hospital gown. A tray of medicines and instruments was scattered across the floor. She was alternating swinging her arms and holding her head.

"Teague. Tell me what's happening. What's upsetting you," Dr. Hansen said.

"I can't. I can't."

"Okay. You don't have to get back in the machine, but you need to calm down."

"I can't. I can't." She didn't look at them or seem to hear Dr. Hansen. "My head. My head hurts."

Dr. Hansen tried to catch Teague's arm to make her stop pacing and face her, but Teague swung around, flinging Dr. Hansen against the wall.

"We're going to have to let security in," Dr. Hansen said.

"No!" Baye lunged after Teague and wrapped her in a tight hug from behind. Teague twisted and dragged her a few paces, then stopped as Baye kept the pressure on her.

"I can't." Teague's resigned tone cut into Baye's heart.

"It's okay. I've got you." She kept her grip firm against Teague's tense body. "It's going to be okay. I didn't mean to hurt you. I didn't understand. I thought I was doing something good for you, but I know better now. I'll never, never deceive you again. I love you, baby. I've been in the pit of darkness without you. Please, please let me back in."

"Baye?"

"Yes, baby. It's me. I'm here. I love you. I never meant to hurt you. I didn't understand. I won't ever do it again."

"I don't want to die." The words were so soft, Baye almost couldn't hear them.

"You're not going to. I'm not going to let you. I love you too much."

"My head hurts."

"Dr. Hansen is here to give you something for that. Will you let her?"

"Okay."

Dr. Hansen moved to them and quickly injected the sedative. "She needs to lie down," she said. Baye loosened her hold and steered them toward a gurney that rested against the wall by the door.

"No," Teague said, her words slurring a bit. "I need to finish." Her eyes drooped, and her legs suddenly went wobbly. Baye slipped next to her, drawing Teague's arm over her shoulder to support her. "I have to know."

Dr. Hansen signaled the technician to come back into the room, and the three of them helped her back onto the bed of the MRI. By the time she was settled, her eyes were closed, and she was limp. The technician fastened straps across her body.

"Pull them snug," Baye said. "The pressure will help keep her calm if she wakes a little."

"Baye." The whisper surprised her, because she was sure Teague was sound asleep.

"I'm here, honey."

"Love you."

Baye didn't try to stop her tears for the words Teague rarely spoke. "I love you, too…so much. Rest now. I'll be here when you're done and will take you home. Then I'll be there with you tomorrow and the next day and the rest of my days if you let me."

Epilogue

More than two years later

Children gathered by the fence to feed slices of carrots and squash to the goats while an amateur magician made balloon animals and his wife painted the faces of another group of kids.

The largest group of children and moms was gathered around Tommy, accompanied by Flower, Snow, and Cappie. Cappie, wearing a tiny cowboy hat and bandanna, rode in a small saddle strapped to Snow's back. Tommy handed out small bites of fruit or nuts that Cappie snatched from the children's hands when they offered them to him. Asset was harnessed to a small cart filled with children as TJ led him along the path Teague and Baye still walked each night. John and Buster presided over a temporary outdoor pen full of puppies and children, and Libby was entertaining a similar group in the cathouse. There were also hot dog and ice cream stations for whoever was hungry.

Heavy Petting Rescue Center had become a popular venue for parties, and today's event was the combined birthday of three children, with almost two hundred parents and kids attending. Besides the fee for hosting the party, a lot of children asked for donations to the center in lieu of presents.

Teague sat nervously on the side porch of the farmhouse, Mac on a perch beside her. She still wasn't comfortable around crowds but had gradually begun participating in the events Baye arranged. If the pressure became too much, she and Mac would retreat into the house. For now, several children stood on the porch, awed by the talking parrot.

"Ring Around the Rosie," Mac sang. "Hello. Pretty. Where's Pretty?"

"She's in the cathouse," Teague said.

"Here, kitty, kitty. Here, kitty, kitty," Mac crooned. He liked performing for an audience.

The children laughed. "Does he understand what you say?" one of the older boys asked.

"Parrots are very smart," Teague said. Reciting knowledge was in her comfort zone. "Researchers have found that they can recognize colors and names of things and solve puzzles. Did he understand what I told him, or did he just respond when I said cathouse? Who knows?"

"Here, kitty, kitty," Mac repeated, then cackled when the children tittered again.

"We're having a party, Mac," Teague said to him, warming to the small group. "What kind of party are we having?"

"Happy birthday to you," he sang. "Happy birthday to you."

The children laughed again, and Mac continued.

"You look like a monkey, and you smell like one, too."

This remark brought belly laughs from the group of kids, and Teague smiled. She'd taught Mac that, much to Baye's consternation.

Baye emerged from the cathouse, spoke to a couple of the parents, then walked quickly toward them.

"Pretty, Pretty," Mac said when he spotted her.

Her smile was broad as she came up the porch steps. "Hey, kids. They're getting ready to sing and cut the cake. You should go over to the birthday table."

"Bye." The children waved as they hurried down the steps. "Bye, Mac."

"Bye-bye," Mac said. "See you later, alligator."

Baye leaned down and brushed her lips against Teague's in a quick kiss. "How are you doing? This is a big crowd."

"We're comfortable here on the porch," Teague said.

"I think things will wind down. I'd ask if you want a hot dog, but I know you're stuck on pasta right now for dinner."

"You don't have to eat pasta every night with me."

"I know. Connie and I are having fish tacos while you eat your pasta."

"Okay."

Baye smiled that smile that always warmed Teague inside. "Are you going to eat it tomorrow, too? It's your forty-second birthday, you know."

The past two years hadn't been entirely smooth for the two of them, but they still saw Dr. Hansen on a regular basis to work out whatever problems came up. The MRI that had brought them back together came back with a clean report, and Dr. Hansen had managed to find the right medicine to stop Teague's headaches. TJ was leaving at the end of the school year to pursue her own career, but Baye had already recruited and trained another student to take her place. She gave up her bedroom in the farmhouse since she lived with Teague, and Libby had turned it into a sitting room for her so they could convert the downstairs living room into a reception room for the center.

Baye had discovered Teague's relatives who succumbed to the Maxwell curse were all male, so she grudgingly let go of the notion that she would die young. And they married in a small ceremony after Teague discovered the estate could pass to her spouse, who would then have to will it to a Maxwell heir if they didn't have children. And they wouldn't. They were happy with their house full of animal kids.

Everyone had returned to the farm, except Miss Abigail, Tater, and Tot. Miss Abigail had turned out to be the boss of the entire herd, and her kids seemed happy in the company of the other goat kids. So Teague rescued a few more goats from the auction that Snow and Lucky could stand guard over, along with the Fluffies.

Life was still a journey, but a good one.

"I will eat pasta," Teague said. "But I will have cake, too." She stood from the chair she'd been rocking in. "I am going to take Mac home. Do you need me to come back and help?"

"No. The cleaning agency's going to take care of all of it. They'll even take down and return the tables we rented so people could sit down and eat."

"Good. See you at home."

Baye kissed her again. "I love you, and when tomorrow comes, I'll love you even more."

Teague smiled, rewarding Baye with an affectionate glance. "When tomorrow comes."

About the Author

D. Jackson Leigh grew up barefoot and happy, swimming in farm ponds and riding rude ponies in rural Georgia. She has retired from her career as a journalist, but continues her real passion—writing sultry lesbian romances laced with her trademark Southern humor and affection for dogs and horses.

She has published 17 novels and one collection of short stories with Bold Strokes Books, winning five Golden Crown Literary Society awards in paranormal, romance, and fantasy categories. She was also a finalist in the romance category of the 2014 Lambda Literary Awards.

You can friend her at facebook.com/d.jackson.leigh.

Books Available From Bold Strokes Books

Blood Rage by Illeandra Young. A stolen artifact, a family in the dark, an entire city on edge. Can SPEAR agent Danika Karson juggle all three over a weekend with the "in-laws" while an unknown, malevolent entity lies in wait upon her very skin? (978-1-63679-539-3)

Ghost Town by R.E. Ward. Blair Wyndon and Leif Henderson are set to prove ghosts exist when the mystery suddenly turns deadly. Someone or something else is in Masonville, and if they don't find a way to escape, they might never leave. (978-1-63679-523-2)

Good Christian Girls by Elizabeth Bradshaw. In this heartfelt coming of age lesbian romance, Lacey and Jo help each other untangle who they are from who everyone says they're supposed to be. (978-1-63679-555-3)

Guide Us Home by CF Frizzell and Jesse J. Thoma. When acquisition of an abandoned lighthouse pits ambitious competitors Nancy and Sam against each other, it takes a WWII tale of two brave women to make them see the light. (978-1-63679-533-1)

Lost Harbor by Kimberly Cooper Griffin. For Alice and Bridget's love to survive, they must find a way to reconcile the most important passions in their lives—devotion to the church and each other. (978-1-63679-463-1)

Never a Bridesmaid by Spencer Greene. As her sister's wedding gets closer, Jessica finds that her hatred for the maid of honor is a bit more complicated than she thought. Could it be something more than hatred? (978-1-63679-559-1)

The Rewind by Nicole Stiling. For police detective Cami Lyons and crime reporter Alicia Flynn, some choices break hearts. Others leave a body count. (978-1-63679-572-0)

Turning Point by Cathy Dunnell. When Asha and her former high school bully Jody struggle to deny their growing attraction, can they move forward without going back? (978-1-63679-549-2)

When Tomorrow Comes by D. Jackson Leigh. Teague Maxwell, convinced she will die before she turns 41, hires animal rescue owner Baye Cobb to rehome her extensive menagerie. (978-1-63679-557-7)

You Had Me at Merlot by Melissa Brayden. Leighton and Jamie have all the ingredients to turn their attraction into love, but it's a recipe for disaster.(978-1-63679-543-0)

Appalachian Awakening by Nance Sparks. The more Amber's and Leslie's paths cross, the more this hike of a lifetime begins to look like a love of a lifetime. (978-1-63679-527-0)

Dreamer by Kris Bryant. When life seems to be too good to be true and love is within reach, Sawyer and Macey discover the truth about the town of Ladybug Junction, and the cold light of reality tests the hearts of these dreamers. (978-1-63679-378-8)

Eyes on Her by Eden Darry. When increasingly violent acts of sabotage threaten to derail the opening of her glamping business, Callie Pope is sure her ex, Jules, has something to do with it. But Jules is dead…isn't she? (978-1-63679-214-9)

Letters from Sarah by Joy Argento. A simple mistake brought them together, but Sarah must release past love to create a future with Lindsey she never dreamed possible. (978-1-63679-509-6)

Lost in the Wild by Kadyan. When their plane crash-lands, Allison and Mike face hunger, cold, a terrifying encounter with a bear, and feelings for each other neither expects. (978-1-63679-545-4)

Not Just Friends by Jordan Meadows. A tragedy leaves Jen struggling to figure out who she is and what is important to her. (978-1-63679-517-1)

Of Auras and Shadows by Jennifer Karter. Eryn and Rina's unexpected love may be exactly what the Community needs to heal the rot that comes not from the fetid Dark Lands that surround the Community but from within. (978-1-63679-541-6)

The Secret Duchess by Jane Walsh. A determined widow defies a duke and falls in love with a fashionable spinster in a fight for her rightful home. (978-1-63679-519-5)

Winter's Spell by Ursula Klein. When former college roommates reunite at a wedding in Provincetown, sparks fly, but can they find true love when evil sirens and trickster mermaids get in the way? (978-1-63679-503-4)

Coasting and Crashing by Ana Hartnett. Life comes easy to Emma Wilson until Lake Palmer shows up at Alder University and derails her every plan. (978-1-63679-511-9)

Every Beat of Her Heart by KC Richardson. Piper and Gillian have their own fears about falling in love, but will they be able to overcome those feelings once they learn each other's secrets? (978-1-63679-515-7)

Fire in the Sky by Radclyffe and Julie Cannon. Two women from different worlds have nothing in common and every reason to wish they'd never met—except for the attraction neither can deny. (978-1-63679-561-4)

Grave Consequences by Sandra Barret. A decade after necromancy became licensed and legalized, can Tamar and Maddy overcome the lingering prejudice against their kind and their growing attraction to each other to uncover a plot that threatens both their lives? (978-1-63679-467-9)

Haunted by Myth by Barbara Ann Wright. When ghost-hunter Chloe seeks an answer to the current spectral epidemic, all clues point to one very famous face: Helen of Troy, whose motives are more complicated than history suggests and whose charms few can resist. (978-1-63679-461-7)

Invisible by Anna Larner. When medical school dropout Phoebe Frink falls for the shy costume shop assistant Violet Unwin, everything about their love feels certain, but can the same be said about their future? (978-1-63679-469-3)

Like They Do in the Movies by Nan Campbell. Celebrity gossip writer Fran Underhill becomes Chelsea Cartwright's personal assistant with the aim of taking the popular actress down, but neither of them anticipates the clash of their attraction. (978-1-63679-525-6)

Limelight by Gun Brooke. Liberty Bell and Palmer Elliston loathe each other. They clash every week on the hottest new TV show, until Liberty starts to sing and the impossible happens. (978-1-63679-192-0)

Playing with Matches by Georgia Beers. To help save Cori's store and help Liz survive her ex's wedding, they strike a deal: a fake relationship, but just for one week. There's no way this will turn into the real deal. (978-1-63679-507-2)